A LUKE OF ALL AGES

and

FIRE AND ICE

New Lit Books
West Bath, Maine

Contents

A Luke of All Ages

A novella

by

MARK SABA

We are always the same age inside.

Gertrude Stein

Hills blocked his view. They were everywhere: some full of old houses stacked like wooden blocks, others full of trees so green in summer he felt they were choking him. Hills marked every step of his, every ride in the car with his mother. He walked up and down hills to get to school, felt his throat drop as they drove down long hills to places where little creeks ran and branches lay in messy piles during the gray winter. To get anywhere, he had to see it in his head before they'd arrived. You could never see things approaching, because everything was hidden behind hills. And, if what he saw after he'd arrived was a little different than what he'd imagined in his head, the picture in his head was what stayed, what mattered.

It had to do with the hills.

Often they would go visiting. Sometimes they would take the noisy streetcar, and sometimes they would ride in the little blue car. The little blue car took them to more mysterious places, places that had nothing to do with his memory, or what he saw in his head. Those were the most interesting places to visit.

He did not know it at the time, but some of these places he would visit only once, once in his life. Then they would vanish, just as if he had never been there, or as if he had only been there in his head. As he grew older he had trouble separating the things he had seen just once from the things he had seen only in his head. He could never be sure, for how could he have imagined anything, were it not for what he actually saw?

There was once a trip to visit a woman his mother knew, a woman she didn't see very often, if ever. They drove through and around the hills. They left the city with its red and orange brick roads, its bumps and breath-taking spills when the roads dipped. It was a breezy day. His sister was at school—another mysterious place that held some kid of magic, a magic adults spoke of with reverence. After turning another bend, his mind lost in the tops of trees, they drove up a small hill that was a parking lot. On either side, connected buildings fell down the hill like big steps. They had brown roofs that sloped down onto the buildings like upside-down, open boxes.

Inside there lived a woman with a clear voice and short, dark hair. She and his mother hugged and kissed, and told him the woman was a friend of his aunt who had died, his mother's sister. Then they did the usual visiting thing: sat down at the kitchen table to drink coffee and talk.

The mention of his dead aunt's name—Celine—made his face go blank. Luke, his mother said. Luke. Here, Dolly has something for you. A toy. A dented metal, swirling top. He pumped the handle up and down and the top swirled, its yellows, reds, and blues all coming together into a swirling cloud as he thought of his Aunt Celine.

He was still in love with her. He saw her coming down the stairs in a dark dress that moved when she walked. She was excited, smiling, holding something she wanted to give him. Her smile made her black eyes light up: her wavy dark hair shining against her shadowy skin. She handed him the gift.

She handed him the gift.

She handed him the gift.

He ripped open the paper and she helped him open the white box. Inside it were pajamas that looked like alligator skin. For him! He looked at her stooping beside him with her smile, her smiling black eyes. He was in love with her. Then she was gone.

He had no sense of how or why she had left. All that remained of her was the box with the alligator pajamas.

Now she was back. She had a friend, a woman with short dark hair and a loud voice who had mentioned her name. Where do the people you love go? Do they always stay inside your head, so that you see them over and over?

Sometimes he went into the books they read. *The Owl and the Pussycat,* a big book with a green cover and big pictures inside of the two of them riding together in a pea-green boat. How calm the water was under moonlight. When he was in that book he couldn't feel anything else, just the nice boat and all the colors from the book floating around him like jewels. Later he would make friends with the *Hardy Boys,* exploring caves with them, solving mysteries, spying strange neighbors.

He picked up most of these books from the library, a small library in a yellow-brick building that sat across the street from his doctor, whom they went to see every week.

Dr. Stendhal was a cruel, smelly man. He smelled like the absence of everything: the absence of warmth and comfort, the absence of good food, the absence of fun, the absence of what he imagined to be a father. And to top it off, he showed absolutely no expression while torturing Luke with his needles and cold metal instruments.

Illness was something Luke didn't really mind though, because it made him feel a little special. The nuns at school sent home tidy little packets of work for him to do, and he completed these tasks with ease. He was sick more often in the winter. That's when he couldn't breathe, when coughing fits kept him up most of the night. His mother said Dr. Stendhal's shots would help him, which was the only reason he suffered them. The long drive down to his office, along the busiest road he knew, passing foreign city neighborhoods while catching glimpses of more distant neighborhoods among the hills, had a calming effect on him and his coughing. There was so much to see, and so much to think about. What went on in all those oddly-shaped buildings? Who lived in all those big old houses with the wide front porches? Who was buried in those sloping green cemeteries? And most importantly, how did firemen manage to shove their wonderful red, yellow, and white trucks into those little garages? He knew that, when they went to see Dr. Stendhal, other kids were at school, which meant that only he could see all that went on in the world while his classmates were imprisoned.

That was magic.

How could he not feel that he was somewhat different? It was not only because of his illness and the fact that his father was dead, but because he felt the world flipped its mesmerizing pages, it seemed, for only him to see. Every night, following his prayers and his mother's kiss, he saw those pages flipping endlessly in his head. It didn't matter whether they showed good or bad things, whether they made him smile or shudder: there they were, every night, just like one of the many books he read. Only better, because he didn't have to read them. They read themselves to him.

During his wakeful hours he saw them too, and of course they competed with the new things he was seeing and hearing, so that the present and past were always colliding in his head. Luke, Sister DeLellis would say. And he would look up and give the answer. She never knew that he was living in two worlds at once. It was so easy to do—why did she look surprised?

The world of adults was many worlds too. Each adult brought a different world to him: different feelings, different smells, different words, even different colors. There was Mrs. Fisher, the neighbor who lived in a dark brown house with an overgrown, brown yard. Luke had never seen her, but it was widely known among neighborhood kids that she was a witch. No matter what kind of day it was—even the most beautiful start of summer vacation in June—dark trees shrouded her house. Most often he ran by it.

Sometimes adults were like ships approaching in open water; he didn't know if he would survive them. But most often (except for Dr. Stendhal) he did. Visitors from his mother's very large family included great aunts dressed in flowers, great uncles red-faced and smelling of beer, cousins who were allowed to have dogs, and most lovingly, his only grandfather.

Grandfathers are another kind of father. In fact, they are fathers themselves. They could be the father of your father. But Luke had no father, and his father's family (he had heard of them) occupied only a distant corner of his mind. It was his mother's father, then, who embodied all he knew of that word.

His grandfather's world was the earth. His skin was dark like the earth. His eyes were the color of twigs. Once, while they were sitting on the front porch one late-summer evening, a hummingbird flew by them, then hovered over the zinnia patch at the base of the steps. Luke was amazed, speechless and ecstatic. But his grandfather only showed a little smile, saying, *He's going to fly all the way to Mexico for the winter.* So there they were, connected by a little bird to exotic Mexico, the same Mexico that had fashioned his grandfather's cane, a whittled stick that was brightly painted with animals. How had he gotten it?

On Sunday nights, after one of his grandmother's long dinners and maybe a game of kickball in the street with the neighborhood kids, he and his grandfather would announce what they were going to see: gazelles, lions, buffalo, elk? Termites, honey bees, eagles, wolves? Other times they would watch the channel where men went fishing, where they caught fish bigger than Luke, hanging by their gills from the fisherman's hands.

Beginning in early spring they would descend the long stairs to the concrete basement, where his grandmother did laundry, where a rack in the middle of the floor stretched out her zig-zaggy afghans, where his mother's cousin (who lived on the second floor) brewed beer, and where his grandfather kept a whole big family of ceramic pots, peat pots, fertilizers, watering cans, and seed packets. Luke smelled the early lives of vegetables and flowers there. He smelled the whole world there, and everything it grew, by the magic of his grandfather's, and his own, hands. Together they planted seeds, mixed strange concoctions of manures, kept notebooks to track their successes and failures. In the end, as summer approached, they carted all the plants outdoors, where Luke, under careful supervision, became his grandfather's hands. He transplanted tomatoes, peppers, cucumbers, broccoli, and cabbage. And earlier, when the air was still cool and the ground just started to give way, he planted seeds directly into the ground: lettuce, peas, radishes, beets, onion sets, and even potato spuds. Their garden, which sat directly behind the garage, found protection by tall hedges on two sides. In the next yard the Stambroskis grew grapes.

There were other worlds, other adults whose lives intersected with Luke's: the man who raised tropical fish and sold them to him for 5¢ each, the man who spoke another language and raised pigeons in a hillside backyard-full of cages which he let out to fly around the city and return, the neighbor who raised canaries, the neighbor who raised plums and cherries, and the grandmother who ran the little store at the top of the hill and dropped penny candy into a little bag for him to fish through during the long walk back down to his grandparents' house.

Each of these souls froze in Luke's imagination. Often he called them up to think about them, about how their lives were so different, about how many lives were even possible in the world, each one making up its own. Together they all seemed to fit together, though. As if Luke were walking through a storybook. All the pages were there: the ones he couldn't stop seeing at night.

At night he heard a train passing through the hills, out of sight, its long whistle finding its way up through the woodland hollow, then up the hill of his backyard, through the window, to his ears. It was often his lullaby, something he wished would never go away.

When he was a bit older he and his best friend, Jerry, investigated that hollow, plumbed its secrets, walked along the creek for hours until they felt sufficiently lost on their excursion. They caught crayfish and salamanders along the way, outran vicious dogs, hacked through elephant ears nearly as tall as themselves, swung on hanging vines, and kept an eye out for poison ivy, which lurked everywhere. If the Willow Street boys wanted to come along, they shunned them, preferring to keep this adventure to themselves. It was a grand thing for a couple of ten-year-olds. Perhaps they would find the infamous Indian Falls along the way, which some of the older neighborhood kids had mentioned in passing. They longed to see the rusty red water that fell there. There might even be arrowheads lying about.

Once they ventured too far, far beyond where the hollow emptied out. They took a turn up a farmer's bare hillside, through a small grove of trees, and saw a tiny wooden house in the distance. Two grown collies ran out to meet them, barking but wagging their furry tails. Luke and Jerry froze. They won't hurt yins, said an old voice in the distance. The boys looked up and spied her rocking on her wooden slab of front porch.

Bertha, as she was named, cheerfully called the boys over through her many missing teeth. She asked them if they liked the dogs, and said the two collies didn't always get along. Would the boys like to take one home with them? It would be okay to go home and ask their mothers and then come back later for it.

Luke put his arms around the lighter dog—a nice, tan color—and felt its coarse fur give way to warmth and a distant heartbeat.

NO! said his mother, and he knew there would be no use in pleading. *The doctor said no pets. And I don't want to clean up after it.*

But I can help…

No!

That was the end of Bertha and her two beautiful collies.

Luke sits and wonders: whatever happened in between? All those years, like rungs on a ladder. Now he was sitting on the top of the ladder, waiting, with his head in the clouds.

Actually he was sitting in a long, quiet room, a room that backed up on the rest of the hillside house, but which opened up by a wall of window to the summer deciduous woods on the other side. His dog, Snuff, slept at the window, taking advantage of the occasional wandering ray of sunlight that poked through to warm him.

Luke sat there feeling fine—that is, nothing much bothered him at the moment. No arthritis in his knees, no unreasonable bills, no insufferable solicitors, nothing to repair, no lingering nightmares, no indigestion, no palpitating heart. He even wondered, in this fortunate state, whether he was alive, alone in his dream house, a house that had become a repository for dreams that had come and gone, though never a vessel for brewing new ones.

Before building his house, Luke had seen it in his mind for most of his adult life. It sat snugly on a forested hillside, neighborless, long and low, with a slanted roof. You approached it from one end, where a simple square door, painted red, anchored its grayish square wall. That wall was all you could see; the rest of the house reached into the woods, like a misplaced barrack.

Luke had planted next to nothing around this entrance. A gravel driveway led up to it, and the rest was anything that wanted to grow on either side of the driveway—above, behind, and below the house, whose nondescript color and elegant form had a calming effect on anyone who visited.

The house contained two floors, though the second floor was more of a loft, with small rectangular windows high up on the downslope side, and no windows on the upslope. For windows, the great common room could not be matched: it rested in the far corner of the building, opposite the entrance, and not only the downslope wall but also that end wall were all glass. This is where Luke often sat, sometimes doing nothing but looking through the glass into the forest, as if he had become a tree-dweller.

Visitors, having entered through the red door, found themselves in an intimate, circular vestibule, dimmed but for the light pouring down from a circular skylight, a light that showed suspended dust motes above a stone table. The table supported a bowl hewn from the same rough granite. The bowl, depending on the season, might contain small flowers floating in water, dried herbs, incense, colorful leaves, nuts or wild fruit. Of course, it made people pause, and reflect, before moving on to the rest of the house. Just as Luke had intended.

Every morning Luke opens his eyes he feels a little bit afraid, afraid because he never knows which world he will be stepping into when he gets out of bed. Will it be the world he most recently remembers (from a dream), the more familiar world he has stepped into countless times before, or a more distant world, one he knows nothing about? Most shocking is when he passes by the mirror, because the person he sees there might not resemble the one he has in his head, the one whose world has changed once again.

The world he often awakens to is not peaceful. It is the same world that appears peaceful when he looks out the window. But it is a very big world, the whole world, that sits up in his head. And it is anything but peaceful.

He awakens only minutes before the alarm goes off, considers for a moment that he must have some kind of supernatural sense of time, then dismisses the idea in favor of a hot shower. He takes his robe off its hook and heads toward the bathroom, but stops a moment: in the soft distance he hears the unmistakable cough of croup. All during his shower he re-evaluates the coming day. Will he have to make a doctor's appointment for his son, find someone to cover his meeting at the office, even take a sick day to stay home and prepare chicken soup?

His wife is out of town. But no matter. He has dealt with this before. When he comes out of the shower he finds his six-year-old standing there in his pajamas, coughing and rubbing his eyes, amidst the steam. —Good. That's good, Luke says. Then he puts on his robe, wraps his son in a towel, and carries him outside, to the February cold, where they stand together for a minute before going back inside.

Is there chicken in the freezer. Might he drag Ivan to the grocery store if not. Is there anything beside the meeting he would be missing. Could he also change the light bulb in the hallway today, fix the buffet drawer that sticks, clean out his sock drawer. And why exactly is his wife so cheerful when talking about the guy on retreat with her at the board meeting?

Ivan's cough worsens to the point of inspiring panic. In another minute or two Luke will be on the phone with Doctor Malvais. But then Ivan nearly gags to death, succeeding in bringing up a glob of mucous into Luke's steady hand. Still, there is a slight fever there, along with those black circles under his eyes. Just who is that guy anyway?

Later, Ivan is asleep under his blanket and two cats, the chicken soup is boiling, and Luke is doodling on a little pad at the kitchen table, trying to work out an idea for a new vodka ad campaign. He's going for a new look, but not too new, as his superior cautions. People don't buy things that are too far from their familiar comfort zone. What bullshit.

Sara the cat, by the way, needs her rabies booster. Is that something he could schedule for late afternoon, if he can get an appointment, and Ivan is up to it?

The doodles merge. He scratches them out, then throws the whole sheet away and starts over. What do they actually do at those board retreats anyway? Sit around in a circle and play Truth or Dare? Flirt? Talk about their spouses? Share desserts at dinner? Why was she so intent on buying those new outfits for this trip? And why do they always go to those resorts, where everyone is walking around relaxed and horny?

That's the problem when you have a strong imagination. It doesn't know when to stop. But it also keeps you going. Every hour of his day brings a new re-organization, the shifting planes of his multi-layered life allowing new perspectives to emerge, letting old ones fizzle and die. Can the cat wait another week or so? She's an indoor cat anyway. Does vodka always have to be in a neutral box, could Ivan be getting strep, does it ever matter how many socks you have, will he dream about his wife tonight?

And so Luke's day unfolds, unpredictably, as always. Luckily, for him, it doesn't matter. He has grown used to uncertainly; he equates it with being alive.

Somewhere, near the end of the streetcar line, there loomed a city. This was the city that could never be seen unless you were in it. Because of the hills. Everyone talked about the city. Many of his mother's friends actually lived there, and he had been to their houses. But there was a different part of the city, a big scary part, that was always invisible. One day they saw it from the streetcar. First, they walked and walked up a big, steep hill. The streetcar waited for them at the top of that hill. His mother pointed out their house way over in the distance. They had come that far!

Streetcars don't make a sound when they first move; they just glide, then they start to rattle, and if you're lucky, sparks fly off the big fishing pole attached to its roof so that you are riding with lightning. Luke couldn't keep his eyes from the window, though they burned from both excitement and fatigue. So many different stores went by, so many people and cars. And then the streetcar went down a long, wide hill. It shook and rattled; sparks flew; the bell rang. At the bottom of the hill they followed a very crowded street. People got on and off. They swung wide and made for a bridge, a special bridge made for streetcars. Below them brown water swirled. On one side of them a giant black furnace burned, sending out orange and yellow smoke. On the other side he saw the tallest buildings he'd ever seen, just like those in *The Wizard of Oz*. That was Pittsburgh, where he lived. Though he had never seen it until now.

He fell asleep—the gentle rocking of the streetcar, his mother's lap, and the hum of conversation among the passengers sent him off into his own darkness. Then, in what seemed like no time at all, she nudged him. *Come on honey. Time to get off.* Where were they going?

A warm breeze hit his face after they said goodbye to the streetcar. They were in a new neighborhood. Pittsburgh had disappeared again. She took his hand, and together they walked down streets full of cars and people. They headed for a little park, walked through it, and ended up on a new street. This one had bigger houses that didn't touch one another and yards to play in. At one house a grandmother stood, wearing a black dress. She was waiving to them. Luke and his mother walked up to meet her.

The woman put her soft, warm hands around Luke's head and bent over to kiss him many times on the cheek. She smelled good. Then she kissed Luke's mother; her voice was like a song and Luke couldn't always understand her. But she brought them into her house, where a lot of people stood up to meet them. Luke felt very happy there. It was a big, warm house and he smelled good food cooking.

After the meal he fell asleep again in someone's lap: another old woman, his other grandmother, who smelled like the sun.

They had planned to build this house, he and Leah. They were always planning, talking and planning. That was when they lived in the neighborhood, the nice pre-war neighborhood with sidewalks, 3 or 4-bedroom homes, their church nearby, girl scouts selling cookies, leaf bags piled up on the sidewalks in fall. And while they were planning, things happened. Ivan grew up. Winter dumped snow. Moles tunneled through the yard. Leah lost her health.

It began, quite simply, with a cough. Now a cough was something that was second-nature to Luke, who had grown up with asthma and every kind of allergy. Along with it came endless throat-clearing, sniffling, and watery eyes. It was hard to image life without a cough. So at first he was barely aware of Leah's, who had also developed seasonal allergies, though not until middle age.

They had met when very young, still in high school, though their schools were at opposite ends of town. She was tall and energetic, like one of the modern figures on pedestals that were sprinkled about the new wing of the art museum where they met for Saturday morning art classes. Her hair was long and unruly; she wore round glasses. They were to work at the paint table that day, filling hundreds of little ketchup cups with basic colors for the rest of the class to use when they came up to the balcony to paint after the lecture. All students had to work at the paint table at least once a year.

Meeting her was like stepping inside himself. He felt free of worries, free of pretense, free of expectations, free of his past. They drew looks from the prefects because of their laughing. On a wide sheet of paper they painted a checkerboard, and used black-and-red filled paint cups to play checkers. The morning passed swiftly, and from then on they sought out each other to sit together during the lectures. Though Leah was often late.

Now, with her illness, Leah looked more beautiful than ever. Her pointed and gregarious personality had softened a bit, allowing him to look more deeply into her green-gray eyes. When she touched him, he felt things pouring out of her that he hadn't felt before. And he knew that, as their time together drew to an end, each second would be magnified more than the previous, until the last second, when time would cease to exist. That thought gave him solace. For then he would be able to find her again on certain mornings, as soon as he had awakened from that other timeless state, sleep.

Luke walked from room to room, following the declining light. It was a little journey he'd taken so many times before. And yet each round he made brought him something new, unforeseen, as if he could never get to know his house fully. He lived alone in that house, but everything in it was imbued with Leah, with Ivan, their pets. A vase she had watered, a drawer she had pulled open, the pan she had fried eggs in—each time Luke laid eyes on them they were transfigured, like talismans. And when he touched them a flood of images poured through him, each from one of the thousands of days they had spent together, unique days, masterpieces every one.

At first he found this unnerving. Then he became used to it, and finally he settled on embracing it. For what was a world of things, if things had no meaning?

Here is a morning in November, a cool morning in the apartment they had lived in: four rooms, a crooked hallway, light flooding in through the dining room's bay window. And Luke steps over a sock, her sock, rolled into a little white ball and lying on the dim wooden floor. The sock is a little reminder for him. It reminds him that she sometimes overlooks things, forgets things, in her earnestness to get through. It also reminds him of her priorities. She would rather get up early on a weekend and go to the café to buy him the almond croissant he likes than stop to pick up a meaningless bit of dirty laundry.

That sock lies on all wooden floors, at all times, but mostly on cool fall mornings in his hillside woodlot house.

At odds with these memorable objects for Luke was a host of objects whose meanings had been foisted on him by a world of commerce, a commerce that had once employed him to design those meanings.

The very things that made his life possible—food, mattresses, books, toothpaste, computers—came wrapped in meaningful logos. They sometimes made his heart jump to see them, especially those that were familiar, favorites that he had been conditioned to believe imparted something good or useful for his randomly hurtful life. The fact that he had spent a good deal of his life creating logos, finding creative ways to introduce useful material things to a harried public, also lent validity to those things. There were, however, times when just about anything he touched or saw in the course of his daily life dissolved into mere comic fluff, grotesque pieces in a board game he must play. But Luke knew, deep down, that life was not a board game. Unless it was a game of checkers.

Some things were too big and scary to touch all at one. One was the hillside building that was his school; inside it were not only two floors of classrooms where the mysterious older kids roamed, but also a church. His classroom was level with the cafeteria, in the basement, though they did have a long wall of windows where he could look out and see pink trees blooming, rain falling, or yellow jackets banging against the panes. The days passed slowly in that room, but they were full and important days, days that taught him how to read, sing, and draw; days that brought a new kind of order to his world, a quiet order that he welcomed.

After a couple of years he moved up a floor: the third grade classroom was there, alongside the library room, where the ancient, little Sister Muriel walked slowly about, rearranging books on their low shelves.

This was a little floor, because most of it was taken up by the church. It was a church that didn't look like other churches they passed by in the car, or like pictures of giant churches he saw in books. But it had all the rules of a church. You had to be quiet while in there, and suffer, and pretend there was nothing else in the world.

Following third grade he became an altar boy. Then he got to see what was hiding in that little room across the hall where the priests got dressed for Mass. It was called the sacristy. The sacristy was really two little rooms put together. When you walked in from the hallway you saw the part where the priest would sit, looking out the long window, thinking. That was where he thought of all the important things he would say during Mass.

To the left was the other room, and that's where everything was kept. Luke's cassock and surplice hung there, along with all the other boys', and the heavy, colorful vestments the priests wore. The room was tidy, with everything in place. Altar cloths lay in drawers; candles came in white boxes that smelled like spring. In that room you would find seasonal things like the censer (for Good Friday, but funerals too), a large crucifix on a long stick, bottles of altar wine, and the untouchable monstrance.

The monstrance held God. It was as big as an open umbrella, made of golden spokes, with a long base which the priest held as long as his hands were guarded by a piece of his chasuble, the loose outer robe he wore. He would carry this monstrance on Good Friday only, holding it high before him by the cloth of his chasuble. In the dead center of the monstrance, where all the spokes met, sat a little window where God lived. To Luke, and to everyone else, it sure looked like just another communion wafer in there. But that host, he was told, was different.

Mass was a little different when Luke served it. When he sat in the pews with his classmates or family he was mostly free to think about anything, but while serving on the altar he had to be more alert, attending to the priest's cues, remaining stock-still, and even on guard at communion time to catch a host that might slip from the tongue of a worshipper onto his golden paten. If a consecrated host touched the ground, there would be trouble.

Certain days in the church were unique. On Ash Wednesday the priest made a dirty thumbprint on your forehead while proclaiming that you were destined to die. On the four Sundays of advent Luke had to remember the exact order of four candles to be lit: three purple and one pink. The pink one always came on the third Sunday, never before. But his favorite church day was the feast of St. Blaise, when the priest held two cool candles crossed at your throat while muttering a prayer. Luke was sure it would one day cure his asthma.

Somewhere in the deep recesses of his brain he remembers it: that cough. But it is only early morning, and his 30-something-year-old's day has not yet begun. That cough was from another time, another place. It was a cough he had outgrown long ago, part of a buried past. Why does he now remember it?

He begins to realize that the cough is not coming from his past, nor his dreams. It comes from the echo-filled hall, where his son sleeps. The cough is deep, hoarse, and unlike any other cough Ivan has had until now. But it is the same cough Luke remembers having had himself, during those gray winter days of his childhood. An asthmatic cough.

Leah is still sleeping. Either she does not hear it, or she considers it less than urgent. Either way, Luke knows he is the only one who knows what it is. Only he knows what this means. In these few seconds, decades away from that childhood illness of his, from the doctor's visits, the shots, the sleepless nights, the burning throat, he realizes that his son will now have to repeat a misfortune that had been cleanly forgotten. This makes Luke's heart beat wildly; he draws a deep breath, and tears roll over his eyes. —Luke, she says, now awakening, what is it?

In those day Luke carried Ivan on his back. He carried him in a big green pack that buckled at the waist. Ivan sat happily at Luke's back, his legs dangling, as Luke climbed the steep hill leading to the nursery. On the way they met a crossing guard who checked to see that Ivan's hat sat properly, or that his pants legs were pulled down to cover any bare skin, or that he looked content sitting in that backpack.

At the nursery they unloaded. Luke presented the staff with Ivan's lunch as they eyed the little guy to make sure he was dressed properly (nothing on backwards or upside down), and Luke was off to work, wondering each day whether or not he would get a phone call from them that Ivan was sick.

During that time Luke's days were filled with little tasks, one after the other, so that the days filled up quickly, flew by; though in retrospect they expanded to fill a brimming psychological past. Luke dove into these tasks one by one, day after day, year after year, never wondering for a moment where they were leading him. He prided himself on being able to keep so many things alive in his head, lined up like duck pins ready for him to bowl down.

One project led to another, bled into one another, spilled onto his pillow at night, made him sing, or bounce Ivan in the air. Plans for logo designs percolated during his drive to work or as he helped Leah prepare dinner; he imagined conversations he would have with clients, phone calls he would make. What he would order for lunch tomorrow. What he would get Leah for her birthday. Life was a quick succession of little doors: open, close; open, close. Why not? It all seemed necessary, necessary and loved.

One could go on like that forever, he often thought. Certain periods of his life had been similar, so full he didn't have time to think, even if he was under the illusion that all he was doing in carrying out these little tasks was thinking. In fact, he was only bowling.

School had been for him the epitome of bowling, unmatched even by young fatherhood. It had required, above all, strategy. He prided himself on being able to determine the method (unique to each class) of obtaining an A. It had something to do with studying, but not always with knowing the material. After all, memorizing recurrent patterns to aid in solving calculus problems was not the same as understanding why calculus existed at all. How were chemistry, French, Japanese art, and political science connected? Surely they should be, if each of these studies originated on the same planet. But, as Luke found out well enough, their professors unanimously avoided acknowledging that what they professed was generally useless without reference to other disciplines. Thus Luke went along, like everyone else, earning his grades and laurels, moving ahead, and securing his position in the economy.

Trouble was, none of this had much to do with Luke's life, which could and would change focus daily. If there was a snowfall he would see that snow covering his desk at work. It would fall over his computer screen; clients and colleagues would brush it off their shoulders when they entered his office. The sounds of branches cracking and blue jays squawking would supplant the ringing phone or canned ding of emails coming in.

Sometimes (more often than not) Luke would present three or four branding ideas to a client, three good ideas and one not-so-good. And the client would pick the not-so-good one. They paid for it. Paying for a bad idea—that was a part of Luke's world that had nothing to do with Luke's life, his real world.

In his world, not only the weather, but also visions consumed him. Visions came in dreams, but they also came during wakeful hours. They demanded recognition, for they would not budge until Luke had examined them from all angles, until he had dwelled on their origins, their significance, their messages both hidden and obvious.

Some visions came from the past; others from the future. Sometimes they came together, like flip sides of a coin. And sometimes they stayed with him forever. The vision of a little boy, their son, a mosaic of all their ancestors, all their personalities and emotions, staring squarely back at Luke. The vision of the yard he cleared out and planted, year after year, its emerald spring announcing his family's future. The vision of his maternal grandparents' house, its many doorways and mysterious, toddler-height corners; the vision of his grandmother sitting there crocheting, inundated by her home's tragic history. The vision of Luke's woodlot home, its searing simplicity; its affirmation of life's sadness and steady beauty.

These visions were hard to carry, hard to leave room for in Luke's crowded, day-to-day brain. But he welcomed them, because they were outside of days; they provided Luke with compelling reasons to live. They could not be destroyed by the economy. They could never be burned to the ground, never grow old or irrelevant or out of style. These visions, Luke knew, may just well be the only part of him that would carry on after his death, that would never be food for worms or fuel for the cremation chamber.

That was why Luke could sit alone in his house as an old man and not be alone.

For ten years he had no home. He had lived, yes, in apartments, in tiny rooms, with family and friends—sometimes sleeping on their couches—from city to city. But during that time he could not call any of them home.

It happened naturally; it flowed out from the course his life had taken. Home was not an edifice; it was something he carried within him. The places he traveled to either burned or enthralled him, sometimes both, but they were never anything he could call home.

That changed when he began living with Leah.

At once, the place where they slept, where they cooked meals together and embraced in the hallway, became a magnet for Luke. For the first time since he was a child, he would rather be home than anywhere else. Outside, the world he had once been so engaged in, with all its vagaries, continued. The newspapers filled their daily columns with all the latest catastrophes perfectly lined up for everyone to obsess over and feel frustrated about. But not Luke. He still took part in those daily worldly catastrophes, yes, but he knew in the end that they were phony. He knew they had nothing really to do with his life, however much he did his obscure and abstract part to help rectify them.

His life was not abstract; it was wonderfully tangible. It was the pile of unfolded laundry sitting in the middle of the living room floor. It was the sunlight lying on the buffet in the dining room, highlighting its rich grain. It was precisely that Saturday afternoon at two o'clock, lying intertwined on the couch with her, that one hour expanding to fill every one of those he spent drawing logos, or grocery shopping, or washing the dishes.

What was it like to be married? And why were some adults not married? He knew it began with a ceremony, and lots of food. That was a good reason to get married. And there was dancing, and women with their hair piled up smelling like a spray can. They gave you a kiss.

Getting married had something to do with photographs too. In the old days it was the only photograph you ever had of yourself—the one they took on your wedding day. He knew that because he'd seen those old photographs of his grandparents and his great-grandparents in their wedding clothes. For some reason though, people didn't smile in photographs back then.

Now his parents did have a happy wedding; he knew because their pictures were happy. His father especially was smiling ear to ear. His mother was smiling too but she looked a little scared. Was getting married scary?

Married people eventually got fat. By the time they were old, all married people were fat. The husbands drank a lot of beer and the wives ate a lot of cake. They smiled a lot to other people but not much to each other. When their kids got older, in high school, they didn't seem to like their parents, and parents whose kids were that old always looked worried. Did getting married and having kids mean you had to learn how to worry? Maybe those people in olden times were smart and knew what was coming, and that's why they weren't smiling.

Anyway, Luke knew that he would get married some day. That's just what people did.

They had both attended the University of Pittsburgh in the 1970s, a post-hippie time of unattested freedom and experimentation in human relationships. Women were finally able to do whatever they wanted. Men were cut loose as well in uncharted territory, living without a cue from past generations about how to live with women.

Sex was everywhere, as it had always been, but now perhaps more promiscuously and unabashedly. It was generally accepted, without question, that you could act on your impulses, let your emotions spill over into the crowd, and hide your insecurities.

Luke, however, had a problem with this. Intimacy, for him, meant complete trust, not probable compatibility. He knew there were others who shared this view, but they were as quiet about it as he. And so he often felt himself living in a limbo of desire, unsure of himself, and wondering if he had come from another planet.

Not so, it appeared, with Leah. The two of them still relished one another's company, but Luke could not let go of himself, his solitary confinement, to become more intimate with her. She scolded him for this, and he did not understand why: it all seemed beyond his control.

They freely dated others, and eventually life got the best of them. They gradually lost touch. He knew she had had other men, her gregariousness could not sit unattended. He grew more involved in his studies, and his first job, upon graduation, took him to the other end of the country. Her career, meanwhile, blossomed in their home town.

It took twelve years of marriage, and what seemed like another lifetime before that, for Luke to undergo the transformation. He kept looking back, imagining what in his past might have made him feel so differently, oblivious to other worlds, other ways of feeling.

In the past he'd accepted everyone and their actions without reservation, and he assumed that people bore total responsibility for those actions. External influences were nothing but little pebbles being flung at mountains of unaffected free will.

So why now, as he entered his fourth decade, did he feel jealous? It felt like a disease that was slowly eating his brain alive, replacing all that previous trust with a contagion that had been spreading behind his back among all of humanity. And if that were indeed the case, he preferred to be a dog.

It had, of course, to do with his wife. It had to do with all of the traits that had attracted him in the first place: an independent spirit, fierceness, sense of adventure, confidence, and his favorite—a slight recklessness. Well, it couldn't be helped then that he eventually felt he had no control over her.

Luckily, their lives were not competitive: Leah sped along in her own career, an industrial engineer, first dutifully submitting one creative solution after another, then moving toward management before becoming a partner in a textile manufacturing company. She sometimes complained, but Luke knew she loved her work. It sometimes took her half-way around the world, and she kept Luke apprised of all the wonderful meals she had and interesting people she met, most of whom were men. There were extracurricular activities too: partner boot-camp in the Himalayas or the Maldives, complete with "team-building" exercises such as white-water rafting or cross-country skiing. Afterwards—what? Hot tubs? Nightclubs? Luke never got all the details, so he was left to imagine them. Leah praised so many of her male colleagues, their attractive personality quirks, exotic hobbies (fencing, viticulture, glass-blowing) that Luke began to feel very ordinary, bound to his unwavering daily routine, transparent to others.

When did married couples begin spending so much time apart? And was it true that their absence from one another made them grow fonder, or just numb? These were not questions for our ordinary Luke, who could only know what he felt.

So Luke found himself in one of his bubbles again, seeing things as defined only by his experience. He neither willed nor censored these bubbles: they were his life. Nor did they somehow prevent Luke from being engaged in the world; they simply colored it for him, however subtly, like a prismatic, soapy film.

In his young fatherhood bubble Leah had become a facet of his perspective, one of the many parts that now made up his life. Other parts included his son, his job, maintaining the house, and that precious half-hour of day-dreaming time he accrued driving to and from work. That, along with the hour or so it took him to fall asleep each night, provided him fuel for the new insecurities he now faced.

What was the difference between cheating and flirting, between making love in bed and making love with your eyes? Was modern life hypocritical, or healthy because of newly accepted avenues of letting off a little sexual steam? Why shouldn't he and Leah occasionally find themselves on those avenues, like everyone else?

It wasn't that Luke denied the world he lived in, or refused to take part in it, but then again he could not bring himself to ask Leah the question: are you flirting behind my back? Do you have dreams of other men? Have you ever let go of everything you've known and learned, and woken up with someone else lying beside you? Luke could imagine these things, yes, from inside his bubble. But he also felt there was another reality, an absolute one that everyone saw together, one that did not change from day to day, or bubble to bubble. In that reality Luke could never address these questions to Leah. No, it would not make sense for him to do so, because it would throw them both so far off track that neither would ever be able to get back on. They would be lost forever outside of absolute reality, and caught in one particularly unpleasant bubble. That bubble was one of deceit and illusion. Luke didn't want to live there.

So he moved several times daily from one world to another, from fatherhood to husband to caretaker to employee, but always kept an eye beyond these worlds to the one that remained constant, the one that somehow maintained a steady peace in him.

Looking up, he sometimes got dizzy. It had to do with the birds, the way their silhouettes flitted into the sun. It was hard to keep track of them as he fumbled through the pages of his well-worn field guide.

He had always been attracted to birds. As a child he was sure that one day he would be able to fly. He practiced on the windiest of days, running down the hillside next to his house, arms spread wide, wearing a light spring jacket that pocketed the wind enough to nearly lift him off the ground. One day it would happen. And now, as an old man, Luke felt that it had happened. His life had taken flight over the years; he felt like one of the birds. And it made him dizzy.

It's funny, in his early life he never knew just how much he was grounded. It had been a life of boundaries, not only the physical boundaries of the landscape, but the boundaries he sensed every time he met an adult. They let him know just what was possible in life, and what wasn't. It's true, he often heard that, as an American, you could be whatever you wanted to be when you grew up. But so many of those whatevers were missing among those he met; or, at times they existed but in a watered-down, disappointing form.

Luke couldn't help it: while watching those wild, elusive birds he remembered people who had walked through his life, mysterious people who only now lost some of their mystery.

Sitting high up in the branches, like dark ghosts, were the turns in Luke's memory, profiles of nearly-forgotten faces, the worlds they had once presented to him, however incompletely. Or, they shuffled through the leaves behind him, fluttered among the delicate twigs of a young hemlock, reflected light from stones lying under running water.

Women came first to his mind: the many friends, cousins, aunts, and neighbors of his mother. They wore bright faces, accomplished in their tasks of motherhood, house commandeering, community work. They walked with determined strides, their hair always in place on top of their heads, maybe a bit of lipstick, a purse in tow. One aunt told him, finger waving in the air, that high school would be the best time of his life, a comment he remembered with a puzzled look the day he graduated from college. Another, a grandmother next door, grew every imaginable thing in her gardens, and could sometimes be seen hoeing out there wearing only baggy shorts and a bra.

The nuns and lay teachers at his school were another kind of woman. They were simultaneously kind and untouchable, as if they had some kind of force-field around them. Teachers were like that. They knew the right way of doing anything: sitting, singing, writing, asking, answering, coloring, addressing, listening. Without teachers, it seemed, everyone would be lost and confused.

The girls in his classes stuck to their roles, too, reading aloud all with the same smug voice, one that didn't sound natural, as if someone had a gun to their heads. Girls all had to hold their books the same way—piled together in folded arms. Most of them shifted their eyes a lot when talking to you, or they did a little spin as if they knew something about ballet (which of course they didn't). Girls were mostly annoying, but they grew up to be mothers, and every mother was wonderful.

With mothers there was nothing to figure out; everything was clear. All their rules made sense, and you didn't have to learn new ones every year and be graded on them. Mothers also smelled nice—sometimes like flowers, sometimes like cookies, sometimes like soap. They smelled good and felt good when they hugged you, and their voices always made you feel something, even when they yelled at you.

The women who came later broke these molds, or they cast themselves into new ones. This both frightened and excited Luke, who was never afraid of anything new. In high school he found that young women could surprise him daily, their thoughts and actions unpredictable to the point of jaw-dropping thrill. They led Luke into new territory, and that territory spread even wider in college.

He remembered most of all Colleen, someone he had never seen cross. She came from a family like his: hard-working, Ellis Islander descendants, fun-loving, not exactly educated. Her sentences, uttered by a clear, lovely feminine voice, almost always contained a bit of unaffected laugh. You could not have a bad day around her. And what was she doing with her life? Plowing through medical school.

Luke dated Colleen once or twice, but he could never imagine taking it further. Colleen was a mythical fixture among his circle of friends, above the trends of the day but also embodying some new feminist values. She proved that you could do it without a lot of fuss and theatrics. Even when, years later, her fiancé was killed in a car crash, she did not break, but quietly got on with her life.

Luke's adult experience with women was colored by two factors: one was his father's early death, which meant that he'd learned no cues on how to deal with women, and the second was that the post-feminist era, newly forged as feminism, was beginning to cool during the time of his adolescence. It meant that he knew no role in the play, but made the script up as he went along.

He was not alone in this approach. Most of the young men and women he knew were in the same boat, and the seas were rocky. They made up for it by giving each other a lot of room. Mistakes were made; emotions broiled. And everyone survived.

Luke, however, sometimes felt distant from his era. He passionately believed in the equality of everyone, not knowing that many generations prior to his had other ideas about how to treat great swaths of people (women, laborers, Jews, Catholics, Africans, and Russians, to name a few). Thus he approached academics, priests, football players, celebrities, and the women who served him in the cafeteria equally. Most of these acquaintances picked up on Luke's trusting nature immediately and found solace in the little world he created for himself and them. A few derided the situation and looked contemptuously on Luke, though he never returned the favor, and let them stumble over themselves into a pit of suspicion and fear.

Of course, Luke's embracing nature could get him into trouble. It seemed he drew certain people like a magnet. He was not always sure what they were searching for, but somehow it resided in Luke. To the detached onlooker it might have seemed to be a sexual attraction, and Luke recognized this too. But what exactly was sexual attraction? There were may levels and intricacies to it. Luke witnessed them in other relationships, but when it came to his, well, there never seemed to be a prototype. He knew it; he could feel it. So often others (young women as well as men) wanted to open new doors with him, doors they probably never considered opening with anyone else.

It was a burden. But Luke played it well. He played it well enough to glide by many, many friendships that had blossomed overnight, but that wilted that minute things heated up to anything more than Luke-warm. After all, if Luke had slept with every woman and man who'd searched the depths of his eyes to find a connection, he wouldn't have survived. The alternative—celibacy—became all the more inviting.

It did occur to him that there might be something about his looks that was doing it. Yet, when he looked in the mirror he found not an exceptionally good-looking man, but a mish-mash of all his relatives living and dead. His reflection only brought to mind other reflections, or photographs of himself. Yes! He had Uncle Albert's nose. Right—those faint rings under his eyes belong to great-grandma Catherine. Or the exact stance, the way his hips adjusted, could be cousin Jerome. It was an endless task, reconstructing himself, but an enjoyable one. What greater thing than to find in yourself so many others, as if you had all been poured from the same set of molds, varying only by color, or the time of day your were created?

So there he was, of medium height and build, sandy brown hair, eyes of indiscernible color (though somewhat bluish), and a face that reflected too many emotions—this he knew from the reactions he found on other's faces. They could be perplexed, or frightened, by its unusually precocious range.

Still, there was no part of him—forearm, buttocks, eyebrows, hands, collarbone, or lips—that hadn't received a compliment at some time or other. Why?

Everything around him—each table, drawer, throw rug, picture frame—told a story. Every cracked window frame, every striped zebra and gourami in his aquarium. The ceiling light fixtures he stared at while lying on the floor, the creaking wooden steps leading down to the musty fruit cellar, the shiny drapes in the living room with their geometric patterns of aqua and browns. The crib his brother slept in, the large bed they shared later with a mattress so soft they would end up sinking toward the middle by daybreak.

The curtains blowing as a summer storm brewed outside, the humming electric fan with its long, sturdy stand. The excitement a plastic Santa Claus in the cubby window generated: his red nose with a light bulb behind it.

The crickets that jumped through his hands on a summer evening, their beautiful brown color leaving him, playing hide-and-seek. The bed of purple iris and orange daylilies that appeared once a year, followed by mounds of white peonies crawling with ants and wasps.

Each of these told him a story, put him to bed at night with a head teaming with their scents, colors, and sounds. He was in love with them, with all the things he found daily in his life, because they were all he knew about being alive.

The most important things, though, were the things he couldn't see, things he had perhaps seen only once, or things he'd heard about but never seen. Did bluebirds fly through his backyard while he was at school? Did bumblebees sleep under the eaves of their house? Where did Christmas go when the cherry trees were blooming?

Sometimes those things were people—mysterious, forgotten people that others may whisper about, but never discuss out loud. Yet he knew that they had once existed; he was sure of it because his memories of them, however obscure and incomplete, refused to go away. They often crossed his path, taking the place of whatever was before his eyes, making him forget where he was for the moment, so that he lived only in memory.

One of the darkest memories was that of Louise, a kind and gentle old woman with a dark face who lived (he was sure) upstairs. She had given him a gift: a red fire engine with a ladder on its back that he could move up and down. Louise looked on, happy, as he played with it. In that time only he and Louise were there, in the narrow hallway at the top of the stairs, in the place where Louise quietly lived.

He counted, among his friends, the people on TV. He could always count on them being there, smiling, when no one else was. Among them was a pretty woman who liked children. She spoke directly to Luke as he lay on the carpet, telling him stories about animals and teaching him how to make puppets. She once told Luke that he could come visit her; she gave him the date and place where they could meet. Luke told his mother about it, and together they drove all over the city, through tunnels and over hills, to see her. They had to wait in a little line, but once they got to the end there she was, even prettier than on TV. Luke was so happy he couldn't talk. She winked at him and gave him a coloring book, and then a little hug. That was nice. He carried her around then forever:

that pretty woman who looked straight at him and touched him from inside the secret world of TV.

There were members of his family, too, who stayed locked inside his head; people he was sure he'd met at one time but who had faded from the world they'd left behind. At least one of them was dead. He was the brother of Luke's grandfather, and the only time Luke saw him was when he was in a coffin.

The coffin was in a crowded room, a room full of adults in black clothes. He followed his mother closely through the forest of legs, holding her coat. When they reached the coffin Luke was eye-to-eye with the dead man. The adults had to bend over or kneel to see the way Luke did. But Luke could see him better than anyone else, because they were at the same height. His name was Uncle Ziggy. He was very thin, and didn't look at all like Luke's grandfather. This dead person made lots of people come to see him, more people than Luke had ever seen together in one place. Afterwards Luke could see Uncle Ziggy and his coffin forever; he had no memory of how they got there, or where they went after they left; only the dead uncle, at eye-level, in his coffin, surrounded by bodies in black clothes.

Other faces peeked at him, distant faces without voices that would never leave. He didn't even know their names, but often something—a sound, a certain wind, a color—would remind him of them. One of them, he found out, was his father.

His father lived in many ways, even if he was invisible. There was the father he addressed every evening as he knelt by his bed, reciting his prayers. There was the father his relatives sometimes mentioned when they saw Luke, making him hold out his hands, touching his face, their voices going lower, never looking at him directly. There was the father who lay underground at the cemetery, where they went once a year on a beautiful spring day to plant purple, white, and red flowers, then bless themselves before driving slowly and quietly away.

But there was also a more private father for Luke, one not connected to night-time prayers, relatives, or cemeteries. He was the one who popped into Luke's head whenever he wanted—usually in the same way, one of a handful of expressions on his face, doing one of a handful of things. He could be reaching down to give Luke candy, waving goodbye as he walked toward the car, or holding a big camera that blinded Luke with its lights. This was the father that was most alive, that would never go away.

His mother had had two sisters and two brothers, but one of each was dead. The younger sister lived upstairs at his grandparents' house. She was pretty too, but in a different way than the dead sister, not a striking beauty, but a trusting and calm face, like one of the saint's faces at church.

Luke would climb the steep steps to the second floor at his grandmother's and find his aunt's flat: a wide kitchen and three smaller rooms. The kitchen was his favorite place, because that's where he found good things to eat, prepared in a way his mother never did.

This aunt and his mother could bicker, though never in a threatening way. It was clear to Luke that they were very different. His mother always seemed to have her mind made up, while Aunt Carla was always on the verge of making a decision, and you never knew which way she'd go. She also liked to have a lot of pretty things around, knick-knacks and potholders and pictures that had poems printed over them, while his mother preferred everything plain. Luke loved his mother, but he often wondered about all those little poems his aunt had hanging about, or the colors she chose in decorating her rooms, even the clothes she wore. She seemed to belong to a secret world that drew Luke in for a peek.

Luke could not help noticing the color of things. They seemed to shout at him, or douse him with their individual feelings. He could not be indifferent to them.

All colors began at home, whether they reflected the clothes his mother wore, the carpet and drapes, the lilacs and daylilies in their yard, or the shiny brilliance of his book covers. If a scarlet bird spoke to him from the pages of a storybook, or a rich red-brown twig caught his eye on a rainy winter day, they would follow him around for weeks, creating a little, breathless place inside him that filled with awe. He would retreat to that place of his favorite colors when they could no longer be found outside him, and soon he had a bank of colors by which he read everything in the world.

Because his colors came from home, from his mother's house as well as his grandparents' and aunt's, they were intertwined with Luke's deepest emotions. Trust was the faded green area rug in his bedroom; exaltation was the rose light of summer mornings pouring through the window; fear was the muted black-brown in an illustration of clothed mice hanging near his bed; love was the aqua trim of their tan-brick house, because it was in that house that love resided.

Though this private world of burning color was transparent to Luke, he found that adults did not share it. He knew this because of the fuss they made over his coloring. It was natural for him to use ten or twelve colors to fill in a train engine, but his teacher stared at the result as if she had never seen a train before. Then she would take the page from Luke and keep it at her desk. Often she would hang Luke's drawings on the cork board so he couldn't bring them home to show his mother. Then he would find himself staring at them during class, wondering why something he'd made seemed so unfamiliar.

It was funny about the colors—all those wonderful blues, reds, browns, and purples in the Crayola box—they could make him feel okay if he was sad, or confused from wondering about too many things. He could feel them anywhere, always.

Once, when he was a bit older, Luke asked his Aunt Carla about his father. Who was he? What was he like? Aunt Carla lit a cigarette. Her rich brown hair glowed from behind as she stood there before her kitchen window. And then she went groping, like she always did, looking for words and trying not to make a mistake, for she knew this was an important topic.

How differently his mother would have handled the question! She would have wrapped up the answer in two or three short, satisfying sentences, putting Luke into a kind of trance and making sure he looked unworried. But Aunt Carla spoke from experience, saying that not only was his father a kind-hearted man, but he had once or twice defended her from one of her sister's rash proclamations, something not even her parents had ever done. He made everyone feel that they counted, that they were equals. She also told Luke that she had kept a few of his father's belongings all these years—a wallet, a medal, his scapular—and that she would hand them over to Luke when he was older. (How had she ended up with these things?)

Aunt Carla lived by now in a small ranch-style house in a sprawling post-war neighborhood, just a bike ride away from Luke's prewar, two-story home. Everything about her house was different: the darkish, red-brown brick, the more modern open layout, the garage (absent at Luke's), a small, raised pool in the backyard, and the earth tones present in all the rooms. Aunt Carla's complexion was about five degrees darker than his mother's; her eyes were the color of olives and chestnuts. She wore scarlet and lime and beige, all complimenting her shadowy skin. She liked darker furniture, but the house never seemed dark. Luke's five cousins were always running through it to brighten it up, as did their shepherd-mix dog, another thing not to be found at Luke's house.

Now the idea that Luke's dead father's wallet resided in Aunt Carla's ranch house only added another layer of mystery to the folkloric character he had become. Luke imagined what color the wallet might be, what shade of brown? Or might it have a military look of drab gray-green, since he had been in the navy? In the end it seemed fitting that it should be in her house, with its indescribable color and unknown contents, because that was Aunt Carla.

There are times when Luke wonders what is left. How much of a life can be measured, and how? Is it the money you have, the offspring you've produced, the stuff you've collected? Or is it all packed away in a jumble of neurons for no one to see, and then finally disappear, at death?

Luke wonders if others can see it on his face: the years, the loved ones, the miracles, the disappointments, the mistakes. He feels all those things are also part of his house, the house he painstakingly designed and lovingly erected; reflections of him are there for anyone to see. And yet he also feels that the house is an imposter. It can never equal the wealth of images, colors, experiences, and emotions Luke carries around in inside him.

The moment he walks outside, as he gets into his car and heads to the hardware or grocery store, everything changes. The trees lose their protective sheath; the sun crashes though his skin. His life unfolds uncontrollably, like floodwater, among the people he meets on the street, in the checkout line, at the coffee shop. In them he finds everyone from his past, in their mannerisms and smiles, their scoffs and faraway looks.

He finds Leah there, the Leah he had fallen in love with. Her dimmed hair in the moonlight as they walk home from a party. The hours he spent trying to reconstruct her face when they were apart. The way his arms folded about her waist and the way they brushed up against one another as they cooked a meal together in their tiny kitchen.

He finds all the years they spent together: the early endless lovemaking years, the childrearing years, the years of settlement and questioning, the years of her illness, the year of her death. That was the year that engulfed all the others for some time.

Maybe because Luke had always been acquainted with death, for as long as he could remember, he felt Leah's death in many ways. There was the first shock, like an electric wave rolling over him, that made him sick and apathetic. Food became a nuisance; sleep provided no rest; others drifted in and out of his consciousness, as if he had no control of his ability to communicate with them. Then a curtain came down and separated him from all the colors, textures, and sounds of a world he had once loved. He was able to go through with the parting rituals, and everyone said he was handling it, but this was only because his life had become suspended animation, a grayness that seemed to creep along on its own, independently of his will.

This lasted for several months. And yet, he did not tire of it; nor did he wish for anything but. The grayness gave him comfort, a respite from the noisy, sensory life he had once led. He remembered feeling this grayness once before, as a child, and thought it must have had something to do with the deaths he had known back then—so long ago, yet still vaguely familiar.

Luke emerged from that year like a perennial plant arriving from dormancy, feeling the freshness of the seasons again, his wound healed, though scarred.

Luke's son was somewhere out there in the world too, making his way, creating his own history, leaving a trail among those he met. Sometimes Luke would forget about him, as if he'd never existed. He'd forget that he'd changed his diaper and coached his soccer team, or that they'd spent so many hours together doing nothing. And then something, someone, would remind him, and Luke would freeze for an instant as if he'd gone through a worm hole in deep space.

Could Ivan be Luke? Was it possible that he would experience everything Luke had experienced in this life? It wasn't a question you could ask of anyone, let alone your son, because it would be as good as asking them to describe the color blue. And of course there was a good deal of stuff Luke had seen and felt that he would never wish on anyone, even if he had learned from it. Would Ivan learn the same way? Would he see and hear the same things, or pass them by on his way to a world that Luke would never know?

How to let go? It was a strange thing to let go, to be relieved that someone should no longer be under your care, but to miss the care you had provided. All Luke could do now was imagine what his son's life was like. What thoughts did he have while bumping through life? What combinations of colors, sounds, and feelings awakened unique enthusiasms and respect for each day? And most importantly, how would Ivan respond to the feelings he had toward others? What wounds would he receive, and how would they keep him in balance, render him an adult?

These were the things Luke thought of while outside his home, running errands in the same world his wife and son had lived in, surrounded by others whose features and mannerisms provided endless reminders of the two people on earth he had loved most.

On his 75th birthday Luke went out to buy himself a birthday cake. He didn't often crave sweets, and cake was something that had to be exceptional for him to eat. So he headed for the one bakery in town that met his standards. He would buy whatever looked most appealing, certain that any choice would suffice.

Though it was a damp and rainy November day, Luke felt good. His litany of aches and worries had subsided, it seemed, for this anniversary date. And Luke had no qualms about turning 75, because he was still on the younger side of octogenarians, and he was over being wistful for younger days. It had taken him this long to feel comfortable with himself and everything he had or hadn't done with his life. Why fret?

The bakery, early as it was in the day, still had much to offer. There was the inevitable chocolate mousse filled with raspberry jam, an assortment of flavored cheesecakes, a vanilla layer cake topped with shaved almonds, and then something a bit unusual: a cake made of chocolate and vanilla layers, garnished with candied pears and hazelnuts, with a butter-cream icing. He took it. The sweet, plump girl with a pierced eyebrow wrapped it up for Luke in its deep white box, securing it with tri-colored ribbon. He picked it up gleefully and headed for the door, where he took one step over the well-worn threshold and feel onto the sidewalk.

His inclination to pick himself up quickly, brush his sleeves, and be off was thwarted by the unwelcome realization that he was indeed a 75-year-old, and that nothing could be done so quickly anymore. The cake appeared to have survived (if the unflattened box was an indication) but it became all too clear to Luke that his body hadn't come away as clean. He couldn't get up.

Repositioning himself did no good: everything hurt, no matter how he turned. It seemed he had been lying there for ages before he realized that someone was speaking to him, as if through a cloud. —OK, sir? Here, grab my hand. And then someone else was behind him, holding him and lifting him about the waist. His legs remained wobbly, but he was able to lean on the young man—no, it was a woman!—who had lifted him.

In no time again they were all back in the shop. Someone brought a bag of ice wrapped in a towel; another, a small cushion for him to lean his head back on. A glass of water appeared on the table beside him, along with an assortment of cookies. Had he gone to heaven?

But in heaven there was no pain, and pain he felt in every joint and muscle, with every turn of his head or shifting of position. Mixed in with the pain though was a sense that he had somehow awakened, that his little accident had brought him closer to his own life. How was that possible? Hadn't he been alive for 75 years now? How many of them had he really been living, and how many spending in hibernation?

Luke looked up and saw the faces of the bakery crew: round, reddish, middle-aged faces; young, brightly lit faces; faces on male and female bodies of varying height—all intent on saving him. Why?

The world was full of them: people who took your money, washed your car, set out your groceries, wrote the books you read to your children. It was impossible to live without them. And yet, as a young man, Luke was constantly running, trying his best to avoid spending too much time with them, when he knew all along that most of the hours in a day were spent with them. And this was the hard part: he enjoyed this interaction, even if it meant taking time away from his career and family pursuits.

Luke had a special talent. He could get along with anyone, thought never for political purposes. He simply enjoyed the interaction, the fascination he had with the seemingly endless permutations of human looks and personalities. The drug store clerk, the mother of his best friend, the dentist, the man who waited with him for the bus—all exerted a certain power over him, drugging him so that he could no longer reason out his life. The effect was merely sweet surrender, a surrender that defined most of his years, as the more abstract achievements of his career and station in society piled up in a feeble show, paling in comparison to the daily thrill of meeting people.

As it turned out though, the older Luke got, the less his life was consumed by these random interactions. They were replaced more and more by the feeble show, the rank and laurels he'd obtained, which sank into an abyss the moment he'd obtained them, and left him melancholic. Was life, then, meant to be melancholic in old age? Were people programmed to become so jaded, so independent that precious few others were of any practical interest? But this was the thing Luke had sworn, as a young man, that he would never do: become so comfortable with himself that no one else could possibly matter as much. He would never pull the plug on life's surprises, for they always came attached to individuals.

As a child Luke once thought: I will be 42 years old in the year 2000. That is not so old. Maybe the new century will not be such a big deal after all. His grandparents were already way over 42, and they were okay. They could still walk, and cook, and yell at each other.

Aunt Carla liked old photographs. She had photos of some *very* old people hanging up, and when Luke asked her who they were she said they were his ancestors. They dressed funny. One of the women wore a cake on her head, tied with a black ribbon. A man had whiskers that spread all over the bottom half of his face, so you could barely see him. In another photo a young couple were dressed for a wedding. The woman wore a hat that looked like the one people wore in the electric chair. —Who are they, he asked. —They are your grandparents. Why did people change?

He played the rest of the day. He and his cousins ran through the yard in the heat, kicked a blue plastic ball, raided a robin's nest, and chased lightning bugs until their eyes ached. And as the light dimmed he noticed what none of the other children seemed to notice: they too were changing. Their faces receded into the dusk and began to look like the old pictures on the wall. Luke sat down on a concrete step. He knew that one day they would all be grown-ups; they would no longer play together or call one another or live down the road from one another. It didn't make Luke sad to know this, but he must have worn a lost look while thinking it, because his favorite cousin, Kim, came over to see what was the matter with him. He shrugged. —I don't know. Nothing.

And off they went to collect more bugs.

The cake sat in his refrigerator for a long time—could it have been weeks? It was not until Ivan came to visit, one chilly evening, that it was discovered behind a jar of pickles, still in its white box.

Ivan pulled it out, opened the box, and began cutting a piece.

—Don't do that, said Luke.

—Why not? (He had already taken a bite.)

—I don't know how old it is. It's from my birthday.

—That was just last week.

Last week? His birthday? But didn't he feel as though he'd aged another five years since then? Wait. He should find a photo of himself that someone took on his birthday, and compare it to the face he saw in the mirror now. But, oh yes, there were no photos of that day, a day he had almost forgotten, because it had been obscured by pain.

That day had started an era, an era of cold darkness that crept into Luke's heart. He had been denying it until Ivan arrived, unannounced, to steal something good from the refrigerator, just as he had done as a child and teenager. Now Ivan was a bright light that moved about the room, a light of purpose, a light of holiness, a light of eras gone by. Could only Luke see them?

Each of the eras Luke saw contained a different Luke, a Luke that differed not just by appearance but by less tangible qualities. Chief among them was the way Luke thought.

It took many eras for Luke to realize this: he could change his mental processes, become a cranial chameleon, due to necessity or just plain boredom. Most often it was beyond control. Eras had no definition unless they were past, and new ones could spring up at any moment, even while you slept.

In one era Luke was a model student; a listener, obedient, responsive. He ingested new concepts like candy, and they tasted just as good. It was an area defined by boundaries, and Luke felt safe inside them. It was an area in which everyone learned to think the same way, give the same answers, and know where they stood in the hierarchy of intelligence. This was school.

Then, after a giant wave had come over him from the direction of hormones, Luke began to ask more questions. He began to see more than one answer for those questions. He disagreed with accepted answers; he cared not for the hierarchy of intelligence. This new era required more than study from Luke; it required him to think about his relationships with others more deeply, to take responsibility for them. Friends became tests for him as surely as vocabulary quizzes. He read new acquaintances as if they were passages from books. His days became calendars, each filled with routines that he had written himself. It became clear, in this adolescent era, that Luke could no longer depend on the grades he received at school as a measure of success. The new success was a mix of grades, appearance, status, and female conquest. In this era he thought, and acted, in increments, never delving too deeply into anything, because there was never enough time.

So it surprised him, some years later, that his brain began to respond differently to long works of fiction, or other creative works. He began to inhabit them again as he had as a child, letting the life he had known falter and recede. His schedule collapsed, along with any order he'd previously found in the world. But the new world—of art—was even more enticing, because it took parts of the old, familiar world and shed dazzling lights on it, so that it shone with colors Luke had never before seen. This was an era of letting go, and he was surprised that it had come so unannounced. Why hadn't they told him this would happen?

Then came the child-rearing years, and his brain collapsed once again. Its vital functions remained, but the depth of its cognizance began to resemble a telegraph more than a well. He became more efficient than he'd ever been, not only completing a wild variety of tasks set before him daily, but excelling in a way he had not thought possible. It was a bit exhilarating, though he did long for the days of total intellectual immersion, before minutia ruled his life.

And where did Luke find himself now, in old age? Did Ivan's visit re-awaken an earlier era or two? Could he now live in all those previous eras at once? Or was he numb to all of them: an empty shell?

Ivan had come back from a long trip; he liked to take trips, whether for business or pleasure. Luke could see them in his face: the adventures he'd taken, the subtleties of expression he had learned from other cultures. It was nothing to travel these days, though Luke, but it was something to be a wide-eyed traveler, to return a different person. Ivan had been forging world-wide bonds for years now, and returning to share them with Luke.

But this time was a bit different. Luke had no interest in learning about Ivan's trip, and Ivan sensed this. This time Ivan had crashed through a time capsule and landed in Luke's kitchen. Luke was confused. Where was the toddler Ivan, the era of soccer and baseball, the awkward adolescent, the confident graduate? All were lost, foreigners who inhabited only photo albums. Life was new again for both of them.

They knew their conversation that night would lead to Leah, and what she had meant to them. Not that they had never spoken of her, but it had usually been in jest, to cheer one another up or assert themselves over the power of grief. Now time had passed, and they had exhausted all other avenues of dealing with her death.

—India's changing, Ivan began. It's looking more and more American.

—How so? said Luke.

—I don't mean McDonald's. I mean values. The way people approach living. What they do and don't do to keep themselves going.

—Workaholics?

—Not everyone. But sure, especially if they're employed by Western companies. And the women—a lot of them are doctors and scientists. They're struggling with raising a family too.

—Too?

—You don't think mom struggled?

—Uh, not just mom.

—You too?

—And you. Luke paused. Well, don't you think?

—I'm not sure. I could never tell. Everyone struggles, and no one knows how they measure up. How can you know if you're struggling any more than anyone else ever did? Especially when you're young. You only know one world—yours. And you think it's normal.

—But looking back now, think. Could we have done anything differently, or better? What if you had to recommend to a young couple the best way to raise a family. What would you say?

Ivan blushed a little, something he hadn't done in a long time.

—I liked that both you guys worked. It was exciting to know that both you and mom had other lives that were so engaged in the world out there, beyond our own little one.

—And what about how crazy things sometimes got? Did you ever feel slighted?

Ivan paused again. —I don't know. It was normal for me. If I felt rushed or anxious I certainly didn't blame you or mom. I would rather blame school, or testing boards, or the Department of Motor Vehicles. Organizations that existed only to torture young people. No, I didn't blame mom at all. But…

—What?

—I have to say I did miss her. Even though she wrote us little notes and called us if she was away, and I knew I could reach her anywhere. But I didn't blame her.

—And if you ever have a family?

—If what?

—How will you manage?

—Just the way you and mom did, I guess. One day at a time.

—But aren't there things you know you'd like to change?

—Those are things I might have changed in my world of thirty years ago. How could I know if they'd apply to a family I might be raising in the future?

—Hmm.

—Okay, I'm being too abstract, I know. I'll tell you this: you and mom sharpened my senses. I think I know what's important. What matters is your sense of priorities, not a scorecard of how much time you spend together. I would pass on that sense to my kids. Besides, every generation is different, right? Who knows what problems I'll face? Or what ones will disappear?

So much was a blur.

Not so much a blur as a familiar sense of longing. Longing for sleep, for a ready meal, for a chance to think, to stop, to walk. Longing for so many days. Years. That was an era, a very long one.

At first Luke saw the parallels between his son's life and his own childhood. That thrilled him; it was like being reborn. A surprise. He never lost that feeling, all through Ivan's childhood. But it was hard to hang on to vitality. His energetic youth calmed to a low hum.

Another surprise was this: no one seemed to notice but him. His work flourished; his parenting was exemplary. Ivan's soccer team won the championship. Their house and yard: flawless. Colleagues, family, and friends noted Luke's cheerful willingness in everything he undertook. Even Luke was inspired by Luke. So why the inner numbness, the longing, the willful uncertainty? It was as if he were watching himself act in a film, wondering who had written a script that he longed to write himself.

Leah played a part in that film. She was more than a prop: she propped everyone else as well. There were days when Luke dragged himself home at the end of the week, sour and disenchanted, and Leah would light the candles, put on the haunting piano music, and open the wine. In a couple of hours the world would disappear. This was something Luke could never manage to do on his own, a gift he gladly accepted.

Or, he would sometimes find himself thinking about her during the day, about the days they had spent together before

Ivan was born, the days before he understood things like performance reviews, multitasking, and retirement funds. Memories could keep him going, it was true, even when he doubted that the memory machine was still strong enough to generate new ones.

But those were the same memories that pained him later, because he almost always lost the battle of trying to see them in an unbiased light. The warm fuzziness of them too often obscured the bleeding wounds they might have caused. But of course, the memories themselves were bleeding warm fuzzy wounds when he experienced them, and that's what made them stick.

In a fatherless house all things are equal. There is no tension between parents, no opposing, gender-based points of view, no one to play favorites or be the object of a child's devious trickery. A boy growing up in such a house will find no competition or limit to the ways he will discover a painfully uncertain world. Each step of his will be self-guided and full of insecurity, but in hindsight the tracks he lays will be more solid and glistening than those laid by others. Luke is that boy, saved not only by his mother's love but also by his love for the things of the world, the things he finds there in dazzling color and texture, every day. Luke played on no town baseball team, but he did play in an overgrown lot on hot summer evenings with the neighborhood boys. Luke found no one to encourage his budding sense of curiosity and passion for asking why, but he did find that these traits could sustain him in moments of spiritual seclusion.

There was a quiet consistency in Luke's life, simplicity, an order born of misfortune but never of pity. He came home, on hot summer evenings, to the hum of a rotating electric fan whose breeze wrapped him gently while he slept. And when he awoke the next morning to the bluish light he knew there could be nothing but discovery to fill the empty day.

At a young age Luke learned how to wash the dishes, to put a room in order, to vacuum, and to weed a garden. He did these things because they were a necessary part of living. Later he would also learn how to cook; but until then he relied on his mother's meals, which ranged from fried baloney sandwiches to fish sticks, from "city chicken" (skewed chunks of veal and pork, breaded and pan fried) to stuffed cabbage and pot pies. All were good; all were served without fanfare but with consistency. Meals were another necessity of living.

What else did you need in order to live? You needed snowy nights when cars passed by wearing their musical chains, which meant school would be cancelled the next day. You needed fireflies, elusive and free, filling yard after yard. You needed a cool rug on the living room floor on which to lie with wet hair after taking a bath, watching TV. You needed one extra curricular activity: fun, and that contained nearly all of life, the thing you used as a proving ground for anything learned in the classroom.

You needed firm but loving hands to hold you, no matter whose hands they were; you needed thunderstorms and lightning; you needed cherry and apple blossoms blowing in the wind; you needed two feet and a bike to get you anywhere; and you needed to know that everyone else in your extended family, your friends, and neighbors needed all these things too. When life was filled with seasons, the only surprises came as ideas, ideas that could bloom in fertile, anchored ground, and never be seen as a threat. That was Luke's world too.

In their time nothing was ever expected; you made life up, naturally, as you went along. If there were role models it was never cool to acknowledge, much less follow them. Boys and girls, in adolescence, both wore heavy, frayed jeans and T-shirts. Hair too became indistinguishable between the sexes: longish and chopped unevenly, like an inverted artichoke.

Still, Luke was able to fall in love. He fell in love with the scent of a girl's hair, with the hint of delicate jaw line that showed through unruly hair, with soft hands and a firm waist. He fell in love with their voices, their lips, their defiance. And when he reunited with Leah in his late twenties, he found all these things again. That was the Leah that could never go away, the one he always came back to.

He had sold just about every one of his belongings—his bed, book shelves, dishes, bicycle, and drafting board. He broke his lease, threw away his running shoes, replacing them with a new pair of ankle-high, black Reeboks. They would be good for walking. And he would be walking for the next three months, at least, through Europe.

After that, he had no plans. Would he stay there, find work, become a vagrant? Or return to Pittsburgh, using his childhood home as a temporary shelter until he got on with the next stage of his life? California had become stale for him, mildly predictable, cold. He knew he was molting, but he didn't know where his new wings would take him.

One week before leaving he received a phone call from Bryce, a friend from his college days who still lived in Pittsburgh. Bryce said he had run in to Luke's old friend Leah, and that she was getting a divorce. Luke had not spoken with her in six years.

He knew she had married, yes, and all along he pretended to believe she had done the right thing. He had wanted to get on with his life, refusing to let the loss overcome him. But he also knew beyond a doubt that he had never let her go, that he would compare every woman he met with her.

So, when she called him two days after running in to Bryce, Luke reacted without thinking. Her voice soothed him all over again; he invited her to Europe, saying that she sounded a bit down and worn out. Did she maybe need a little vacation? He knew, right after saying it, that he had made a fool of himself.

But she gladly accepted.

By middle age their lives had taken different turns. Their careers had blossomed in distinct directions, consuming most of their time. And what little time was left was consumed by Ivan. There was little hope.

By now Luke had thrown in the towel on life—not given up on living, but willing to compromise his instincts in order to get by. He was tired. He was even a bit irritable. It seemed his days were filled with the most random and disconnected events, often fires he had to put out or school functions he had to attend. He was Dr. Jekyll and Mr. Hyde times a hundred. Nothing took advantage of his full attention, or his full range of talents.

Then it happened. Ivan went off to college, and Luke skidded down the runway of life as its breaks were applied. He had not prepared for it. He had not thought it would make a difference. But it did.

Leah, on the other hand, had been preparing and talking about it for quite some time, and Luke had thought this annoying. Luke had been speeding along in the ever-present, gobbling up obstacles and relishing sunsets. Couldn't he overcome just about anything?

Turned out that Leah, although she had prepared for an empty nest, had no idea what to do to refill it. It was up to Luke. And he was stumped.

So he arranged for them to go on a little trip. He chose a mountain retreat. Leah perused the web site describing it. At first she wasn't sure it would be quite right, then she went along with it, withholding expectations as best she could. They left on a Friday afternoon, just as a light rain was beginning to fall. And half-way through the four-hour drive they hit a bump—a serious bump—that threw the car off the road. Luke steered down to a stop, then hopped out to survey a blown-out tire on the front passenger's side. Leah reached for her cell phone.

—What are you doing?

—Calling Triple A.

—No, they'll take forever to get here. I'll change it.

—Are you sure? What if the wheel's bent or something?

—I don't think it is.

—Do you know what you're doing?

—I've only changed a million tires in my life, I don't know.

—Oh-kaye.

Leah got out of the car. How different it was, thought Luke. How different form the first flat they had experienced together. They had been driving home from a long picnic day—the day after a prom that he had invited her to. They had lain together under pine trees on a bed of needles, numb from beer and sun, until an army of ants began crawling over them and Leah shook them off with such a shudder that Luke broke up laughing. She was only slightly amused, but not yet old enough to consider the event of any importance. After five minutes it was forgotten.

The flat came hours later, the end of a long hot day, when the falling sun sparkled through a curtain of haze and backdrop of gray trees. It began slowly, an almost inaudible thumping. Leah looked up; she lay with her head on Luke's lap as he drove, resting with eyes closed. —Uh-oh, she heard him say. Then she rose: Oh!

From that point they went into emergency mode, as if in a trance, joking as Luke jacked up the car and spun the flat tire off its wheel, his hands blackening. In no time they were off again, laughing as they recalled the ants, the saggy sandwiches, the mosquitoes and muddy water they had swum in. It had been a glorious day for them, one to be etched in memory not as one filled with obstacles but as one they had filled with themselves.

So why, so many years later, did a flat tire become so much more than a flat tire? It presented itself as one of life's gnawing imperfections. Not insurmountable, but jarring enough to make them blame someone for it, the nearest person of course being each other.

But even that could be overcome with oh, even more work. Relationships at this age were no different than life at the office: work, problems, annoyances, and more work. Hard work could give results, however, and sometimes they were so positive that the effort to get them seemed trifling in retrospect.

—It's okay, Luke said. We'll be on our way soon.

—Are you sure?

—Yes. Then he gave her a little kiss, and she relaxed. Just like that.

The weekend grew slowly between them, with walks and quiet breakfasts and little hugs. They succeeded in finding themselves again, without Ivan, as if they had come down a long road in storms and darkness to find a lighted place. This is the way it must be now, thought Luke, the way of middle age, when all things are relative. He was only just beginning to realize the power he had to shape the future.

The child Luke does a lot of walking, walking through neighborhoods, through woods, down long, long steps and up steep roads. If the weather is nice he rides his red bicycle. He loves the color red, the many shades of it he has found in his crayon box. His favorite is scarlet.

New cars come out in the fall, and that's when he and Jerry trek down to the main thoroughfare, the one that leads in one direction to the heart of the city and the other to more distant suburbs. The part they walk to is more like the city, full of tight stores with mostly run-down fronts and oily sidewalks. They sit on a busy corner where cars, lots of them, stop at a traffic light, and they wait. Luke holds a chart he has drawn up. It contains the names of all the new models, categorized by the main companies: Chevrolet, Buick, Pontiac, Cadillac, Chrysler, Dodge, Mercury, Ford, and American Motors. This is a big year. Nearly all of the models are sporting something new: side signals. Luke and Jerry put check marks next to models that chance to pass by, so new and shiny they make Luke's heart stop. After a couple of hours pass they cross the street and drop into Murphy's, where they search out the same cars in plastic model kits, along with little bottles of metallic paint in any color they like.

Once they walk all the way down Burnsville Road, three miles or so, to sit in the Buick and Chevy dealer showrooms, smelling the new vinyl and reading lists of the newest optional features pasted on the cars' windows.

Those were walks of discovery, long walks you never felt until the end of the day, when your legs ached.

In another few years he will be walking to a school that sits on a hilltop across the hollow, behind the rows of houses that cut into that hillside, all of which he can see from the small back window of the second floor of his house, his house on the ridge of another hill in the endless jumble of Pittsburgh's hills. He will walk there on a cool spring morning wearing a light coat, spend the school day staring out windows or at a particular girl's hair, then go running with the track team up and down those hills. They will jog up a hundred steps, find a small length of level road, then on up, down, and up, down again. Their legs will become steel, and they will race boys from other Pittsburgh boroughs whose legs have also turned to steel. And later still, during his first years at the university, he will have more opportunities to walk. He will walk in a hurry from class to class across busy intersections and wide green lawns. He will walk alone on weekend mornings past the great museums and monuments to Pittsburgh's elite fraternal organizations. He will walk home in the middle of the night, when streetlamps made the only humming sound and the air pressed his skin with the newness of a day not yet arrived. He will walk through the oldest neighborhoods, where his grandparents had walked during their early days as wounded immigrants. He would walk in all the times and places of that great, confusing city while falling deeply in love with it, a love that was as painful as it was thrilling. A love that would never leave him, never, until his death.

Funny, as Luke became elderly, he did not want to walk any more. He might start out, take a few steps down the wooded driveway, or choose a distant parking spot in town as he made his way to the store, but inevitably he would become bored and irritated. Everything looked so familiar and predictable. He could not bear it. It wasn't that he condescended to his surroundings; he felt they were condescending to him. What could that line of thin dogwoods know of the thousands of other dogwoods he had seen in his past? And how could the giant blooming magnolia at the end of the driveway ever compete with the one he had passed by at 3 AM when he was twenty-one, having just walked home his love? Any robin could not comment on the one that appeared on the lawn through a veil of rain in March, 1964, as Luke gazed from his window.

The streets changed, but their connections remained invisible, wires that choked their meaning out of existence. Streets filled with the histories of others, each individual's story told through building façades, reflections in their windows, layers of paint endured by endless rain, wind, and sun. By now Luke knew that he held the cards. Nothing was there unless he saw it, and not unless he saw it in his own way. A walk was only as good as a reverie in an over-stuffed chair overlooking the trees. The trees themselves had stories to tell, but their secrets were more intricate, hidden from all but the most astute and contemplative. For what was Luke's life, but a particle, a tiny cell sliding along on a rough planet's surface? If he didn't make sense of it, who would? Shopkeepers and gardeners would come and go, leveling and rebuilding for all time. Luke could not depend on them, nor their works. His only life was that which had lain its colors before his eyes, fleetingly, but most significantly, as its unequalled miracle.

Luke wanted to achieve something. All his life he wanted it. But just when he was on the verge of naming it, time and time again, it eluded him. It lay buried under appointments and accomplishments, under conversations and the gazes of his contemporaries. But it always resurfaced, looking for a name.

Others might have called it peace, or peace of mind. But these too were vague abstractions, prey to greeting card dribble and party talk. What Luke was after was the very seed of elusiveness, the irreducible kernel that gave him something to live for. It contained not only peace of mind, but violence and tragedy as well. It contained not one state of mind, but the inexhaustible variations of mood and perspective that made up his life. Whether he willed them or not. What Luke really wanted was grace—the ability to accept everything in passing, and feel that he had grown into more of himself—because of it.

But why, oh why did it take so much time? At the close of every era of his life, Luke felt a brief sense of contentedness, but this was soon followed by an even greater restlessness than he had previously known. Elusiveness became a hare galloping away from him, then stopping to look back for a moment before scurrying away again.

Luke often noted with horror and amazement the number of individuals he met who had given themselves up to grotesque illusions of *happiness*. He cringed when he heard the word. How could anyone wish to be in such a permanent state which, having no alternative, would cease to have definition?

After winter the whole world looked as if it had been blown dry. A bright sun covered the dust, warming everything equally before anything woke up. Luke could remember this time, a time that made his heart jump with enthusiasm to play in the yard again, to watch the world unfold and know that outside the air felt the same as inside.

After a few weeks, after the tulips had come and gone and the bush with the small white flowers began blooming, they would get in the car and take a long ride down Burnsville Road. The car would go up hills, then down, up, then down again, sometimes following long curves. When he heard the blinker, and his mother put on the brakes, he knew they were about to enter the cemetery.

It was a Polish cemetery, and laid into the brick-and-stone gateway at its entrance were Polish words, strange words full of crooked lines and consonants. Immediately after the gate the car fell down a long hill; there were no graves along that hill, just weeds on one side, and a fence keeping in another cemetery on the other.

At the bottom of the hill lay their cemetery, among wide mounds inside a long circle of road. His father's grave lay a good ways around the circle. They usually stopped near the faucet to fill up their yellow watering can before getting to the grave.

Luke liked to plant things. He dug out a perfect patch of clean dirt on either side of the small, raised gravestone with the slanted face. There, as his mother stood and watched, he set bright red geraniums, small tufts of blue ageratum, and maybe a white petunia or two. He watered them with the yellow watering can, letting some splash onto the stone if birds had dropped their white splotches on it. He might also straighten the metal holder that contained a large candle, or the other holder that kept the little flag straight. It was there, he was told, because his father had been in the navy. Some of the words on the stone had to do with the navy; Luke didn't understand those words, but they had dates with them, and Luke sometimes confused those dates with the dates his father had been born and died. Cemeteries were generally quiet; you could barely hear cars moving at the top of the hill in the distance. Orange brick houses showed here and there behind the trees. In the farthest part of the cemetery some very old, oddly-shaped stones rose through uncut grass like goblins. Luke preferred not to go there.

But often birds clamored overhead, and usually the sun was bright enough to cheer anything up. So he and his mother removed the trowel, the fertilizer, the empty flower pots, and watering can. They pulled any remaining weeds and washed their hands in the left-over water. Then they stood together quietly and said their prayers. Another year had passed.

Looking back, life was so easy. Everything fell neatly into place. All the trials of youth became nothing but small tick marks on a timeline. Each torment alleviated by an obvious decision, the outcome valuable, not matter whether it be painful, easy, or forever vague.

And yet, Luke felt that he still didn't know why he was still standing. Why had he survived Leah, his unimaginative schooling, the crazy drivers on the highway? Yes, looking back each episode of his life made perfect sense. But all together, life didn't.

There was a time before marrying Leah, a time after growing up, but not yet knowing what he'd grown into. That was perhaps the most difficult time of Luke's life. He was neither nostalgic for his childhood, nor much aware of his impending mortality. The only way out of this limbo was by way of experimenting, of trying out one thing after another, so that he could permanently reject things. Hopefully, his life would then crystallize into something he could be sure about. He would leave this tortuous age of complete uncertainty behind. At least that was the plan.

What really happened was this:

He forgot the plan. Completely. What took its place? Days. Days one by one, each hurling surprises at him so fast he couldn't think.

It began with a wanderlust. Luke packed up and set off to roam about Europe, choosing only the most daring countries, most of which were behind the Iron Curtain. At twenty-something, he stayed at youth hostels in the big cities. He also courted the kindness of strangers, and was rewarded accordingly.

Scandinavia was his portal. In Stockholm he found planes of warm colors delineating buildings, and then intersecting a sky purely blue and white. A solstice sun threw sheets of light obliquely over the whole city, its many spires avoiding shadow, and its inhabitants entranced by long days, as if the dark winter had been an illusion.

There he met a group of three Norwegians, one of whom, Per-Arne, resembled a shaggy rock star. Another, Magnus, bore a chiseled face and even blonde hair; he was a weightlifter. The third, Sven, was part gypsy. His skin was dark and his hair was the color of stained fruitwood. Together they welcomed Luke and toured the city with him. Evenings they drank beer and compared stories of their homelands. After three days they parted company, but Luke was sorry to see them go. It was so easy for him to make friends, so easy to slip into other worlds and forget anything that he had been. On this trip he would become many Lukes; he would store and catalogue these Lukes, wondering which, if any, was the most authentic; the one that might resurface in other dimensions, or lead him into adulthood.

Luke had Slavic roots on his mother's side. Russia had always attracted him. Her literature, music, and aesthetic sense drove deeply into his soul, like a gust of wind. Even in its socialist grayness, Russia appeared vibrant to him, its people infused with a genuine sense of humanity.

His tour guide in Leningrad was a smallish blonde named Katya, who always looked as if she had just rolled out of bed.

Her English, though full of vocabulary, plodded along in a strange syntax, as if she had learned it as an extinct language. Luke found this charming.

Katya's eyes hinted distinctly of an Asian ancestry, as did her cheekbones and expressive mouth. But generally she wore a serious look, as if she were always preoccupied, or rehearsing her English momentarily before she spoke.

So Luke went to bed, after three tiresome days in Moscow, thinking about Katya. The soft lace curtains blew about the open window; the streets were quiet, a three-quarter moon shone on the Orthodox church beside his hotel, and Luke fell asleep. He awoke with a bright northern light, still entangled in his dream. But he had not dreamt of Katya; he had dreamt about the Norwegians.

He had grown attached to males before: friends, he called them. They could make him laugh; they could draw him out of himself, and at least create the illusion that his decisions were not his own. So why had Sven the Norwegian been staring at him in this dream, staring without expression, his brown eyes becoming wells that drew Luke in deeper and deeper, until he didn't know why he couldn't look away?

Luke awoke neither wanting to wake up nor go back into the dream. He was in limbo again. How could he dismiss those brown eyes; what message did they contain?

Luke did finally get out of bed. The tour was soon leaving for the monastery.

He sat on the bus next to another American: a bleach-blonde from D.C. who had just come from India and put a small diamond through her nose. The effect was interesting, but lost in the midst of all her whitish hair. Luke knew she had sought him out. But he didn't want to have anything to do with her. His eyes, when straying from the passing scenery, still landed on Tanya.

There was also a group of Brazilians on the tour, young men with dark hair and wide eyes. They brushed up on one another often while jostling for a spot to view the monastery at its gates; they also befriended Luke, and afforded very little personal space when speaking with him. Luke caught a whiff of their bodies and felt a bit claustrophobic when they laid a hand on his shoulder, or brushed by him, in animated discussion.

By the day's end he longed even more for the cool and understated softness of Tanya.

Luke left Russia feeling a bit bewildered, unsure of where the feeling would take him. He rode on a train to the Polish border, where a stout Russian woman in navy blue searched his backpack and pretended to read the scribble in his journal, much to the amusement of two old Polish women in his cabin.

Poland itself spread like sunshine in greens, browns, and gold for as far as he could see. Even the clouds seemed more colorful, deep piles of rose and yellow-tinted sheets torn and billowing through the sky.

He arrived in Warsaw very late. Everything was closed. Where would he sleep? He made his way to Old Town and found an open bar that served him pork in a mustard sauce. From another patron he learned of a hostel nearby; there was plenty of room there. Old Town had only gas lamps for light. The entire quarter had been rebuilt after the war because the Germans had blown it up, block by block, taking care to eradicate every building's foundation. But the people had excellent memories, and they were able to recreate *Stare Miasto* so authentically that even modern encroachments (such as electric streetlights) were eliminated.

So Luke walked doggedly to the hostel two blocks away by gas light, hearing no footsteps other than his own, in this saddened corner of socialist Europe. He was met there by a somewhat reserved middle-aged gentleman, who was preoccupied with keeping an eye on his energetic toddler son. Luke found a bed in a room where two others already lay sleeping, and he shed his outer clothes before climbing in. But he did not fall asleep for a long time, watching the shadows made by a gas lamp outside the window bounce on the walls.

He awoke very early, even though he had slept little, to half-dreams of his childhood. How out of place they seemed! He heard his friends' voices, smelled a vegetable soup his mother was cooking, felt his collar sticking to his neck during a hot Sunday mass. But none of it belonged here in this Polish hostel. What was there, though, to take its place? He would have to get out of bed, and wash away the night, to find out.

That day brought fascination; a loving respect for the soft greens, ochres, and muted reds of Polish buildings; a welcoming feeling among its patient inhabitants; but also a feeling of estrangement, of being condemned always to the status of onlooker. Luke was forever on the other side of the window, watching lives go by, the same lives, no matter the country.

He soon began to feel that he was deleting everybody.

And now, Luke felt more wrapped in himself than ever. He was beginning to know himself too well. Was there more to living? Wouldn't he rather be thrown into the maelstrom, like everybody else? Wouldn't he rather have a unique place in the daily drama he witnessed on his travels? But that was easier said than done. For Luke was nothing if not honest, and this integrity led him where it would, independently of Luke's conscious directing. One thing he knew though was that he would no longer be the traveler. He would seek his part in the play, and accept the part that would be given him.

He couldn't help it: Luke was an observer. Even when taking part, he noticed everything around him. He took in the shapes, shadows, and shades of a frenetic office. He stopped during a late-night walk to detect the darkest blues and palest yellows of the night sky. Ivan's soccer game was not only the success of his team over its opponent; it was the flock of Canadian geese flapping overhead, the wild and disorderly display of parents gazing forward, the poetry of movement in sport, the mosquito buzzing at his neck.

This instinct for observation never left Luke, never, not even when he found himself taking part in the scenery that knocked at his senses. In those days Luke found himself split: one Luke a fleeting piece of the human puzzle, the other a lone figure who could sit for hours in a reading chair, more often looking up than reading, keeping slow account of the declining light and birds darting outside the window. He became very good at splitting himself, for there was no alternative, as long as he was alive.

He would drive to work singing, singing so loud he would miss Leah's call on the little phone inside his pocket. A list of necessary tasks to be performed that day, written on a yellow sticky note, glared from the console. Six projects, all in various stages of disarray, awaited him the moment he stepped into the office. Also awaiting was a voice message from the school nurse reporting the fever Ivan had developed in the twenty minutes since Luke had dropped him off. And the 9:00 meeting he had forgotten about. And the re-organization of the company (now for the eleventh time). And Leah's birthday coming up in two days.

A list in the car, a list at the office. A mental list. A list on the calendar. E-mail. Voice mail. Junk mail. Every waking moment (as well as many of those he spent falling asleep or waking up) was taken by a slot on one of these lists.

But lists are finite, Luke thought. They can only be counted and commodified, and never be anything greater than themselves. When you strike items off a list, the list is dead, as are all the things that were on it. A list is nothing more than a battle plan, and battles can follow one after another for all eternity.

It was much more gratifying, and interesting, to cultivate a sense of eternity devoid of lists and their battles. Luke could do this during the little spaces between to-do items. And since those items were finite, the spaces between them were infinite.

That is why he sang in the car on the way to work. Luke loved traffic jams. If he was not singing he was carrying on a dialogue with the imbeciles on the radio. He mimicked their caricatures, their affected voices mouthing the words to two-dimensional news stories. The false sincerity of the voices advertising false products. The astounding actors who called themselves politicians running for office. All these gave fuel to Luke's infinite spaces; he filled them with song and mimicry, entertaining himself while clearing away the cobwebs that lists had woven in his brain.

At the office, too, he found ways to cultivate the freedom he found between lists. Most of the time it took the form of a smile, a Good Morning, or the advancement of a subtle private joke. These encouraged Luke to finish the day without continuously checking the clock. Often he would meet someone whose life was consumed by worrying about lists when not executing them, and he would try to nudge them away for a bit into the Free Space, but he was not always successful. Though he did, more often than not, see a hint of acknowledgement in their eyes.

The only problem with Luke leading this dual life was this: though he tried his best to draw people into the Infinite Space Between Lists, he more often felt as if he were its only inhabitant. And at some random point while living there he would realize this, and feel its freedom being replaced by darkness. It wasn't always nice. It could happen anywhere, but more often it happened when he was at home, with Leah and Ivan out on one of her many shopping excursions. Luke might have just finished tightening a door knob, cutting the grass and refilling the bird feeders. He would sit in the living room, mid-afternoon, on a perfectly fine and lovely summer day. He would sit there for longer than he could tell, his eyes locked on a semi-distant focal point, and disappear from this world. Then he began to feel a slight tug: back to Earth! And he would of course return, feeling bruised by this small but timeless excursion into the infinite.

In all the years, all the eras and places he called home; all the misfortunes and blessings, the child and the man, there was only one Luke. He couldn't deny it. Nor did he have much choice; that Luke was here to stay.

He would often be shocked when he looked in the mirror. Who is that? Which Luke? It wasn't the one he remembered. Or, it wasn't the one he had conjured up—Lukes that could change as frequently as the rungs he ascended on his ladder toward enlightenment. For no matter which Luke stared back at him from the mirror, it was never the right one.

The One Luke, however, did not exist in mirrors. Nor could he be photographed. His clothes could bear no complements, and none of his family members, friends, or acquaintances could describe him. One Luke was not entirely visible; he existed as a cubist painting, an incomprehensible mishmash of views compounded into one being. He lived in memory as much as the present. Perhaps he had existed before he was even conscious.

This Luke could not have made it alone. Yet he would have fizzled away into others' views of him if he hadn't been somehow grounded in his own reality. Where did it come from?

The space surrounding Luke is sacred; it cannot be altered. No matter rain falling on him, or the stifling heat that envelopes him in summer. He feels the warm light of their little modern church coming in through its many plain windows. He feels the Polish stews his mother makes warming him even as they cook and fill the air with their lovely aromas. He feels the smooth, dry dirt under his hand as he pats it into place at their campsite in the neighborhood woods. He feels, much later, the firm body of his first love, her breath like cherries entering his. He feels his own body pulse following a track race, and knows it is there to bend to his will.

Sleeping in a college dormitory, inside a tent, or in a small inn in a foreign land, he feels these things. When answering an unkind stranger, being grilled by a professor, or rejected by a client, he feels these things. They were what forged the One Luke, sustaining him with their order. Thus One Luke could grow and become stronger, which was strange because he was invisible. By old age all the other Lukes had come and gone; the ones he had seen in the mirror lasted only for the blink of an eye. But One Luke was as comforting as ever. He became the guardian of Luke's whole life; as long as he lived, there were no beginnings and endings, only the steadfastness of that Luke.

He crawled into bed after saying his prayers. Every bone of his body was tired. His legs ached. And his eyelids closed heavily over burning eyes, soothing them so that he had never felt anything so good.

Light was fading fast over the bedroom where he and his brother slept. The air hung still, neither hot nor cold, putting everything to rest: the old chest of drawers, the plastic crucifix on the pale green wall, the thin green spread that covered him, the parakeet sitting on its perch with its head tucked into its shoulder, the unplugged metal fan. Outside, crickets were chirping. And Luke could not see them, but he knew that by now bats darted silently about the neighborhood yards, sweeping up bugs that broke through the softly-tinted evening air. Finally a short breeze lifted the translucent curtains that hung about the open window. Luke felt it travel up his covers and brush his face. It was a cool breeze, the end of summer. But he did not think about what may be coming next; he simply let himself fall asleep.

Between falling asleep and awakening with Leah by his side there was a profound loneliness, the loneliness of dreams. It was the loneliness of being in-between, the limbo of frightening possibilities, a step outside the world he knew. He returned there every night.

In that limbo he knew no one; everyone he had known became elusive. Luke was chained to the post of onlooker in his dreams, watching loved ones come and go. And now he awakens. He feels the wide bed, and knows it contains two. She is still asleep, the curves of her warm body breaking the stark geometry of the room. The covers fold about her like gentle ocean waves. Luke awakens. The room is filled with light.

Outside their bedroom is a long hallway; the hallway leads to other rooms, rooms they have filled lovingly with an array of carefully selected objects: an antique table, brass vase filled with daffodils, pastel-shaded rug, blue lamps, a tall chest of narrow drawers for the baby's clothes, Luke's father's writing desk. Little by little they have populated the once empty apartment rooms. Now the three of them—Luke, Leah, and Ivan—inhabit them. They fill them daily with a history, a history that meets Luke every morning when he opens his eyes.

Leah stirs, and they touch. The hallway, and all the adjacent rooms, become distant. They are marooned on the wide bed, just the two of them, holding one another against the crash of the world. Light overcomes the room, blurs the walls, blurs the day. They make love on a Sunday morning. The church goers still sleep; Ivan still sleeps. The Lukes of All Ages disappear. The One Luke is hidden, waiting to return. But for now they make love, smiting all the things they have bought, wildly oblivious to their histories. They are inside one another now, and the present continues as if there had never been another time, the limbo of dreams as distant as the sky.

Signs of Luke hung everywhere. The things he advertised through his work also advertised him, long after he had forgotten that he'd made them. In the course of his employment he had provided the means to advertise everything from toothpaste to garden hoses, things people needed to carry on in their daily lives, and even a few things people didn't need.

In the course of providing this advertising fodder, consumer objects began to take on a different meaning for Luke. When he shopped, he was able to strip away all the packaging and verbiage associated with the object. Perusing shelves in the grocery store, he no longer saw a riot of tasteless and aggressive wrapping, but the naked items that were meant to be hidden. He saw inside each item, its food colorings, artificial sweeteners, and other chemicals gleaming at him as simply as the elements of the periodic table.

In time he began to see the underlying nature of all things. He found shopping for clothes distasteful, and preferred the windows in his home to be devoid of curtains, drapes, or blinds. In the summertime he rarely wore shoes. When he met a woman (or man) who was excessively made-up he had no trouble deleting eyeliner, hair colorings, jewelry, tattoos, or the results of plastic surgery reconstructions to arrive at the person in all his or her nakedness. He wanted to know people as he knew winter trees and garden dirt.

This was the Luke of forty-something, just beginning to feel comfortable with himself and the way he saw things. And seeing through to the heart of things made him see his past more clearly. Rooms he had known, neighborhoods and meals and views, crystallized into a permanent catalogue of visions.

Most importantly, those he had loved, and who had loved him, came into focus. They appeared luminescent against the darkness of time. Some of them—certain childhood friends—he only realized he loved in retrospect. They reappeared walking with him through alleyways, thrashing a path through woods, catching bumblebees in jars.

From childhood also came vague shadows of old relatives, whose luminescence showed only in outline, as if from the corner of his eye. They were there because they too had loved him. He could not recall their voices, but their warm, wrinkly hands had held him on their laps; he was sure. He remembered looking out for his mother for a moment before surrendering to their protection.

Hovering about his house always were two figures: the one who took care of him, and the one who took him on little trips. Once they went on an unpleasant trip; they drove in the car up a little hill and then went to see a man who took scissors and began cutting off pieces of his head. Luke screamed and thrashed until it was over, but the hovering figure rescued him and took him back home.

The same figure once took him to a place of big noises, where giant machines rose in the air and made a lot of wind. He pointed to the machines, feeling so happy he almost left that figure's arms, but the arms held tight, and Luke knew the noises, the wind, and the giants would never get him.

After a while the two figures became one, and the one that was left was his mother. She lived with him, took him to school and worked at the school, took him home and made dinner, painted his bedroom, and bought him toys on his birthday. That was the love that anchored all the others, those of his extended family as well as those yet to come, loves that would arrive in their many strange and unexpected forms.

As Luke walked through the visible world and found his heart aching for small wild birds and bare trees covered with spring buds, their familiarity made them gradually disappear. All springs rolled into one; every beautiful vegetable garden produced exactly the same vegetables, year after year.

But individuals haunted him. He might have forgotten many of the details that made them up (the words they had spoken, color of their eyes, places where Luke had met them) but still they remained etched in Luke's heart. Their permanence was a result of their elusiveness. How could anyone figure out another person? How could Luke know exactly what attracted him to others? Each of those he had loved was built of a thousand conversations, a thousand subtleties of facial expression, laughter and unending silences that had passed between them. It all added up; together, more than the trees and earth and stars, they made up him.

In Luke's life, all thirty-seven long years of it, he never thought he'd be playing with a blonde, curly-haired little boy, his son. They roll over one another on the carpeted floor. The boy laughs continuously, testing his father's wits, loving this game. Afterwards he wanders off, and Luke follows him.

The boy helps trim the yard. He points out a flower they have missed watering, a twig lying on the ground. In his face

Luke sees all of his and Leah's ancestors, every one, resurfacing
with a slight turn of Ivan's head, or look of curiosity or thrill.
And yet he is none of them; he is himself a curiosity. What will
he turn out to be? What label will society affix to his beautiful
face in years to come? None that could ever describe who he is.
That boy will prove, once again, the elusiveness of love.

How to know Leah? Leah. Leahs. The Leah of his memories, the Leah now gone. Leah the mother of Ivan. Leah whom he made love to every night. Leah who, along with him, vanquished the petty and evil world. Leah who had taken the place of all unknowns, who had sucked the mystery out of living and replaced it with one thing.

Now she is gone. Now everything she had once stood for is gone with her, and what rushes in to fill its place? An old, stale religion: the religion of Luke's youth. A religion that doesn't budge from its place above humanity, that sets rules to follow, scripts designed to anesthetize Luke's mind so that he will forget that he was once able to live without fear and longing. An old Luke no longer goes to church, but the religion is still rooted inside him, offering nothing new to tie together the vast chasms of his life.

Luke lights a candle. He lights two or three candles. He sits in his favorite chair, the one offering a view of the deep woods on the other side of the window-wall. He says to himself, now I am praying. Incense fills his mind; images of saints petrified by their own gazes, gazes that ignore you, see through you, on their way to nothing. His house is a quiet church. Water dripping rhythmically from a gutter echoes as if through a long nave: its drops become a chant. And Luke thinks, have I ever been perfect? Have I recognized my shortcomings, apologized for them, proceeded to do penance for them? What is penance? Is it a quantity, three Our Fathers and ten Hail Marys, or is it a bundle of other words: I'm sorry, I was wrong, I didn't mean to…. Is penance little more than an order imposed on a distant, chaotic past? Of course, it was easy to do penance, anyone could do it. But how would it make any difference for future sins? How would it reach the dead?

It seemed that sins could only be forgiven by the dead, because forgiveness dealt with things from the past, people and situations that were as good as dead. Had he treated Leah as well as he'd imagined? Had he withheld his penance of wrong-doings when she was alive?

But then maybe penance was not a chore. Maybe it was a celebration, a realization that you could be better, a magic puff of wind that cleared the air. Forgiveness that flowed both ways. *It forgive you, my husband Luke! I forgive your oblivious looks in my direction, your negligence in acknowledging my idiosyncrasies, my weaknesses, the ones that required you to be my crutch.*

And I, Luke forgive my wife; forgive her for leaving me here; forgive the daggers that poured from her mouth; the astoundingly insensitive cruelties; the ongoing insecurity that fed them.

A religion of opposites, of co-habiting partners, of parents, of love and resentment and perseverance: this was Luke's new religion. He attended its service in his armchair, overlooking the wild woods, thinking of his human life, a reflection that stared back at him from the glass, and cut him off from the unfeeling brutality beyond.

There she stood, president of the Association of Industrial Engineers. Quite prestigious, he knew. And yet he felt he was acting in another play, this time in a secondary role. And Leah too played a part, stunning everyone with her charm and intelligence. Still, it was but a play.

Luke had become accustomed to acting. It was something all adults did, a way of life, the only way for most. His other life, the real one, would occasionally resurface, mostly when he was in a creative state. He and Leah had met in that state. He knew she harbored it too. In fact, it had been the prevailing state of their generation, their youth. Everything—roles, futures, expectations, interactions—had to be created from the ground up. The black-and-white world of their parents was a joke, while the sepia-tinted one of their grandparents was too distant in its attractiveness to be taken seriously. So they were cut loose, a generation that came of age in the 70's, sandwiched between the Vietnam Baby Boomers and the apathetic Generation X that was to follow.

Living lives without cues, guided by a firm rejection of the past, was difficult. And yet it could also be exhilarating, because every day, if they got through it, could be measured as a genuine success over the chaos of indecision. Who would feed the baby? Who sweep the floors? Who make the money? Who balance the checkbook? The generation of Luke and Leah could not afford to be apathetic, for if they were they would be dead in the water. They knew life only by creating it, one day at a time.

Relic institutions never quite fit their world. They had developed in a time that did not belong to Luke and Leah. They often presented gender codes and assumptions about how to live that would forever feel foreign to them. That is why Luke knew they were both acting at Leah's professionals meeting. True, she had attained a position once held exclusively by men, but she had to act prescriptively like a male to get there. It was an interesting game to play, but it had little to do with living: the life that had brought them together.

After Leah's little speech and the attending applause, she came back to the round table where Luke sat with some of her colleagues. There was little for him to say, for he felt that any ensuing conversation he could have with them would only be an echo of such scripted encounters. This kind of polite, professional, boring interaction wore him out. He felt like going for a swim.

But Leah pulled the script off with such ease that Luke only found her more beautiful. Several times she touched his shoulder as she spoke, or brushed his knee under the table, as if to let him know that she still resided in their world as well.

Later that evening they came home to find Ivan asleep. The babysitter bade good-night and their house stood with dishes in the sink, toys strewn over the living room floor, an opened newspaper on the kitchen table, and a large gray spot on the ceiling where the upstairs bathroom leaked. But they saw none of it, and headed instinctively to their bedroom to consummate an evening that finally belonged to them.

There had been a time that belonged to Luke, though he was not then aware of it. He had considered that time possibly paradise, because he was so at ease with not only himself but also the world around him. He was twenty-two, just finishing his last year at college, alone, but unaware of his loneliness. He was unaware of many things, though he had thought himself full to the brim.

It happened like this:

Luke first sat in a light-filled classroom. His sturdy pencils sat neatly in a pouch under the heavy lid of his beige desk. When he opened the lid, he smelled eraser, his new box of crayons, PeeChee folders, and the brown paper bags that wrapped his books. Everything in the room had an appointed place: the letters circling the room above the green chalkboards, the stack of papers on Sister's desk, the window ledge wiped clean and supporting neat rows of books she had not yet given out, the crucifix above the doorway, the portrait of Pope Pius. It was as if a clean wind had blown through, relieving the room of dust, or sadness, or of anyone else who had been in there before Luke's class of fifty. Sister DeLellis blew about the room in her white robe, the large wooden beads of her rosary dangling from her waist, helping everyone in turn with their writing assignment. This was the beginning of what Luke considered to be paradise: learning. It was almost as good as his mother's vegetable soup. This paradise lasted through sixth grade. By seventh grade his hormones had firmly kicked in, and he began to wonder if paradise could be found somewhere else. For example, in girls.

In this early adolescent interim he could still be captivated by a story, a painting, or an algebraic equation, but he did not find his attention undivided again until college. There he ingested whole kernels of thought from so many others, each offered to him without reservation or condition. He took them and built a palace inside himself of reason, creativity, and logic. He assumed everyone harbored these vast and decorated rooms. How was it possible to live without them? And he did find a campus full of those who shared this sentiment. Then he graduated, and the world came crashing down on him.

For one thing, there was so much wrong with it. Not wrong on a grand and obvious scale, but wrong on a daily, minute basis. He could not take for granted that others would value his enlightenment, especially if they themselves had never experienced anything of the sort. They were only trying to get by, easing the pain when they could with junk TV, junk food, drink, and the company of others who did the same. Deep in his heart Luke knew they were not to blame, but he also feared very deeply that he would lose everything he had gained at school. The world as classroom was so much less forgiving. There was no way to prepare for it. And worse, it was the world he had been raised in, the world of his only family.

His mother, long remarried, lived in the same six-room house he'd grown up in, only by now it had been transformed by a steady but tepid step-father. Everything was in perfect shape, though its perfection had more often been arranged hastily, according to his mother's whims. The result, not unlike a department store showroom, was devoid of sensitivity. Luke had to live there now, as he frantically searched for the next phase of his life.

The neighborhood, following four years of college, had been eerily transformed into a two-dimensional movie set, even if he knew it was inhabited by deeply three-dimensional characters. He saw it on a new scale: everything in it was tiny, its childhood vastness and mystery vanished. He saw people living to get by, steady in their work, steady by their families, steady in their bee-lines to the grave. It was maddening. Didn't they know there was more than this?

Luke's isolation grew. He quarreled with his parents, even when he noticed the bewildered look on their faces. He would go for long drives to nowhere, investigating the city's neighborhoods, those he had seen as a child, and those he had not. From his vantage point he was able to tie them all together, to loosen the divisions he had once felt from their caged inhabitants.

At one point he dropped in to see his great aunt, the one who had never married. She lived with her widowed sister in a row house in the city's Polish neighborhood, a tidy matrix of narrow streets under the shadow of a soot-blackened behemoth steel mill. Aunt Monica had lived her whole life there, growing up under the care of her immigrant parents, then finding work as a construction secretary, then retiring to dote on her many nieces and nephews. Luke might not have stopped to see her that day if she hadn't been sitting on the sidewalk in a folding chair, fanning herself while waving to the many neighbors who welcomed her cheerful smiles and hellos. When she saw Luke slowing down to wave, she nearly fell off her seat.

She took his face into her hands as if he were a puppy, asked about everyone in the family, and invited him in for a slice of sweetbread, which she made regularly. Her sister, Aunt Johanna, joined them for conversation at the table. And Luke learned much about Aunt Monica that day. He learned that her eyes held a past that fed their merriment. It was a revelation to Luke that great aunts had once been young, and what he heard from his aunt's lips that day, in her quavering, rich voice, bore witness to a young life more adventurous than any he had known.

Aunt Monica had rallied at Pittsburgh's hall of Polish Falcons on April 3, 1917 for Polish independence. In fact, she had helped pave the way. Shortly afterward, she joined forces in occupied Poland to help realize the dream, which indeed came true. She brought out her decorations from the Polish army to show Luke, who sat there aghast. What other adventures were locked in the hearts of sweet old aunts on the South Side of Pittsburgh? What scents, colors, textures, and sounds had Aunt Monica found in a war-wrecked, occupied land? What thrills must have run through her heart, the same heart that she opened every time she laid eyes of one of her siblings' offspring? The merriment that gleamed in her eyes came from a life she had lived with purpose, even if much of it lay hidden in the past. That, too, was enlightenment. Aunt Monica had never gone to college, nor even high school.

Luke felt sick—not a debilitating sickness, but a sickness that made his own foolish heart ache. There were meaningful people in the world, and their lives could never be compared to his own narrow experience, whether it be from books or childhood haunts. Now his life became more complicated. The interior life he had cultivated at college could only be useful in light of a world full of Aunt Monicas, of Polish soldiers dying to resurrect their homeland, of mothers like his who had borne children, each one miraculous and mysterious, into a world they would see with new eyes. All he could do now was get to know that world even better than he had known it, to try to see it from as many sets of eyes as possible. That alone would keep him from feeling distant, the way he felt that summer after he had graduated from college.

Luke felt himself moving in and out of this world many times during his life. He would be engaged deeply, for years at time; then he would detach himself once again, and lose the sense of camaraderie he had developed during those engaging years. How did it start?

In the beginning, he felt himself simultaneously engaged and disengaged. He played with his friends, fought with his brother and sister, and kissed his mother goodnight. Life was like that. But he also found himself staring up at trees, believing he saw figures up there, or wandering what message the sparkling lights were trying to tell him. There were also messages in the bees that went from flower to flower, or curls of fog that wrapped around streetlights. No one else seemed to bother about them. It was during those times of trying to figure out the world's messages that he felt most keenly the loss of his father.

Fathers, as far as he could tell, might help you understand things. They sat quietly in his friends' houses and read the paper, and if you asked them anything they always had an answer. It would save a lot of time trying to figure things out. When he asked his mother questions like why does the air change color, she often rolled her eyes and asked Jesus for help. But Jesus was another one who wasn't around. So there was Luke without any answers.

But that, he discovered, was okay. He made peace with not knowing, and once he did, mysteries poured into him from everywhere and everyone. He felt entrusted to their secret codes. These secrets replaced his absent father. Why not? They looked after him as his life unfolded, just as a father would. He got used to it, so used to it that he simply couldn't understand why others didn't know about it. Why, for instance, were some people afraid of being alone? Why were they afraid to talk about things they had no answer for, like death?

In college he found some fruitful discussion on such forbidden topics, but in the end his friends went back to their idle chatter, their throwaway loves, and their astounding ability to take stock in consensus views of just about anything. They had no use for lights in the treetops or the smell of dawn. Since Luke did, he gradually found that it might not be advantageous to live alone with his observations. In fact, he found others mocking him for it, or worse, accusing him of withdrawing voluntarily from the society of the unobservant, to which everyone, it seemed, belonged.

That was disheartening, particularly when it came to intimacy.

But time came to Luke's rescue, and he went bumping along with his life, though he had a giant question mark inside him that would never recede. It would turn from innocuous white to threatening red any time he was uncertain of himself; it even overcame his best intentions in his relationships with others, and that only helped to prove his "inattentiveness" even more. It was a sorry cycle, one that he lived with for, it seemed, ages.

Then he took a dive. He rejected his interior life, or shelved it, in favor of marriage and all its attending worldly responsibilities. He marched by all those secrets of the natural world, even as they called out to him, on his way to baseball practice with Ivan or the dry cleaners to pick up Leah's suits. At the office he passed up the more human, deeper connections he found with his colleagues in favor of categorizing them into productivity modules in line with his new role as manager. Soon life became a quick succession of time bytes, each of which connected him to other human activity, but which left no time at all for daydreaming, which had once been his specialty. He lived well in those days, a model husband, father, breadwinner, and citizen. But his nights suffered.

Nights were filled with tormented dreams, dark mirrors of the daydreams that had been barred from that model life. He awoke each morning worn out from battle, his exhaustion following him from the bed to the shower to breakfast to the office. Each day he fought to get back to "normal," to begin conversations with others again, to crack little jokes and drink enough coffee to get him out of his sleepy rut.

Trouble is, he longed for those nightdreams as much as he once had for daydreams. They were a sieve, letting everything that was meaningless fall through and leaving only enticing symbols behind. And those symbols gave structure to his life; they made it all add up in a way that his bank account or work performance review didn't. Connections would surface during the day, much as he tried not to let them, tying those dream symbols to what was going on in his life, or what had happened in his past. Each one was an epiphany, making him smile, and ultimately giving him a certain peace of mind, a release from guilt, insecurity, or feelings of inadequacy. It was his bliss.

In time, of course, he couldn't ignore this bliss any longer. He began coming in to work a little later, allowing time to write down his dreams immediately upon waking up. He discussed them with Leah, even if she was too preoccupied to listen. He read books by Carl Jung and others about interpreting dreams, elated to know he was not the only one to revere them.

Living voluntarily with your dreams, both day and night, meant you had nothing to hide. It put problems in perspective. Instead of maddening obstacles, they became puzzles that could ultimately be solved. Even problems that had once loomed over Luke like lumbering zeppelins became small and insignificant in retrospect.

He thought of the preoccupations of his youth. He was too skinny. His hair wasn't right. He did not find the idea of treating others as sex objects appealing. He often preferred the company of animals to their owners. He hated summer, which he considered synonymous with discomfort. Quizzes and tests excited him. A good professor lifted him off the earth. Difficult people liked him. Yet, all through his youth he refused to stay put in the here and now. He would rather design his future, a time when all of his idiosyncrasies didn't matter, when he didn't dwell on the differences he noted between himself and others, but the similarities. This kept him living fully.

The television told the truth. There it was, etched in black and white, rooted on the living room carpet in its decorative wooden box. A man recited the news, a man in a gray suit and a darker gray tie. He never smiled, because many of the things he said were worrisome, about important people dying and other people fighting and buildings on fire. Once he made his mother cry, because the president was dead.

Nuns were also black-and-white, and they knew everything too. Their faces were full of directions, and they never worried about anything. Luke felt safe when they were around. In school he learned why everything worked the way it did.

Each lesson was a building block; the world was made of them. All you had to do was understand everything, and then you would be an adult.

At home, too, he had everything to learn. His mother, his grandparents, aunts and uncles, all those relatives he met at family reunions, teachers, his mother's friends, neighbors—all had rules to follow. It seemed like a complicated mess to him, though all those adults never seemed to be confused about it. They all knew exactly what to do, how to live, what to say to him, how to instruct him so that he would one day fill their shoes. Was it a good conspiracy? In any case, he couldn't wait for the day when he didn't have to figure things out, when he didn't have to spend his life learning the script.

One thing adults often said was that time flew. How was that possible? Clocks ticked so slowly, especially in the classroom. All those seconds—there were millions of them—just dragged and dragged. And when Luke thought of things that happened a long time ago he could picture them so clearly, as if he were reliving them. That made time seem like it could repeat. Doesn't that make it go slower too? The things he remembered came back so slowly, and things that happened now did too, but these were nothing compared to everything that would come next in Luke's life: he still had to grow up, and go to high school, then college, and then get married and have his own kids. And what about being a grandfather? How would it even be possible for him to think about how much time would pass before that happened? Every one of those days he must live would be jam-packed. They would make him hungry and tired. They would make him feel things that might make him cry! Luke could see it in old people's eyes too; they had all lived jam-packed days, and they were almost through with it. Their skin looked like a dinosaur's. It was probably hard knowing all that time.

This is something—Luke's view of time—that never changed as he became older. His days swelled and passed by when he was eighteen, thirty-three, fifty, and seventy-five just the same. They gathered in retrospect like trees fading in the distance over mountaintops on their way to foreign lands, each tree a complete catalogue of emotions, human tugging, confusion, rest, and daily meals. Some trees stood out, but all were alive and fit enough to reach the sky. Together they stood in awe of one another.

It happened occasionally, unpredictably, that Luke was able to step outside of the normal course of his life's events. It could happen at any age, at any time. He might be lying in bed, waiting on a street corner, or cooking a beef stew. A familiar door would open, and he would step into a stream whose water was always the same. It had to do with time, a feeling that it didn't exist, and that whatever Luke happened to be doing at that point was all that mattered. None of the grades he'd earned at school mattered, nor adulations from his superiors at work, nor physical fitness, nor his savings account. All of these would be the same in life as in death. But those timeless episodes gave Luke a glimpse of the universal, a sense of worth in merely existing. It seemed his greatest accomplishment.

First Ivan left. Then the mortgage was paid. Then Luke retired. And then, without warning, Leah died.

Luke, who had swung so many times from being deeply connected to people and things to the ever deeper connection to the unknown, felt himself permanently cut loose. How would he live? By what relative perspective? For the first time in his life, he was frightened of being alone, because he knew that he had arrived at a point which would influence the rest of his life, no matter what he did, or whom he met.

But why, after all these years, should he feel differently? Whatever he thought and felt must come from deep within, like mist rising from a subterranean lake. There was something old in that mist, something that had been there from Luke's earliest days. Why had it become frightful? The arc of his life had returned him there, hadn't it? So much of that life was now distant, almost unfamiliar. Who were all those Lukes during all those eras? Each of them had gone hunting for something, and most often had found what they had gone looking for. But those Lukes seemed inauthentic to the point of embarrassment now. Now, in his old age, Luke found a purity in being without having to go hunting. He had nothing left to find. Words, symbols, and colors no longer worked to anesthetize and deceive others, as they had when he was paid to make them do so. And other humans did not exist to be manipulated or beaten in some pointless game. Those he had loved most were gone. Yet he felt he could love still. He could love being alive, finally, without endlessly planning the next stage of it. How was he able to do this? He saw so many others—others who had attained more riches, had more children, earned honors enough to fill a wall—who could no longer love. Who were miserable to the point of emanating unkindness and remorse everywhere they went. In fact, there were more of these people around then Luke could count. Was he the anomaly?

He had become forgetful. He couldn't remember the ingredients of his favorite dishes, nor the name of his first date. Calendar days all looked the same to him (Tuesday? Saturday?) and common words sometimes slipped from his brain completely before he recovered them days later, usually in the middle of the night. He had no choice, then, but to surrender. If he could not remember everything, everything was not important.

So much seemed to matter less and less, as if his life had been a tightly woven net all those long years, catching only the most vital knowledge and feeling, while letting meaningless drudgery pass through. He felt himself longing for the simplest of all choices: black-and-white television, sparse furnishings, dial phones, one kind of soap (good for hair too), boiled vegetables, and vanilla ice cream. He liked more and more feeling cold in winter and hot in summer, longing for one season's pile of blankets and the other's open windows and grinding crickets.

He also began attending Mass frequently, though he preferred weekdays to Sundays, because on weekdays there was no organ, and only the briefest of homilies. During those Masses he forgot all the perceived injustices of the Church, those he had once preached against. Now all that mattered was the predictable ritual, the candles and colorful robes, the slanted light of church windows, and the brief silences that punctuated the priest's monologue. What did it all mean? He had no clue, but he found it had caught in the net—a necessity.

Necessities were all that concerned him now.

So many things could have a name. All their words piled up inside him; all he had to do was think for a moment to call them up. Tigerlily, Flag, Peony, Lilyofthevalley, Lilac, Redbird, Bluebird, Sputzie, Snapdragon, Dragonfly, Bumblebee, Buckeye. Each of them stood out in color. He waited for them every spring.

But in the background were so many unknowns. Weeds. Did they also have names? Or were they just weeds. Rocks. Why were they different colors? And dirt was not the same everywhere. In his garden it was something like clay and pebbles, but where he and Jerry smoothed out roads for their Matchbox cars it was dry and dusty.

There were also words for how people felt. Most of the time they were happy, sad, or angry. But in between those were a lot of others, and he didn't yet know the names of them. He got into the habit then of not saying anything, because he couldn't name what he wanted to say. Maybe he would learn all words by and by, and then be able to know people better. Maybe it would happen when he was an adult.

For now though everything he felt was complicated. Christmas morning was not just happy; it was a little sad too. Walking home on a cloudy winter day, when little twigs and dried-up leaves blew along with him, made him feel welcomed and bright inside. What was that feeling called? Once he pushed Jerry because Jerry made him mad. He felt scared then, out of breath, then a little happy but mostly like he was walking on air. It was very surprising.

Why did adults keep so many secrets? You could see them in their eyes, the way they looked at one another when you were around. They could name everything without talking! Was this a secret, or was it magic? In those days Luke lay in bed wondering, but soon he gave up and dozed off under the warm covers.

By adolescence he wasn't so lucky. Warm covers weren't enough to drive his thoughts away, nor was the realization that you learned new words by studying them; there were still loads of things and, more importantly, feelings, that he couldn't name. Surely the vocabulary existed. He just had to unearth it, one word at a time.

But he had other things to do, new obligations to churn out good grades in all his subjects, social relationships to maintain, girls to win over, money to make. If he fell asleep at all, it was only from exhaustion.

This young adulthood, unbeknownst to him at the time, set the stage for the rest of his life. It became more and more frenetic, less and less reflective. Words became commodities, their meanings only fodder for capital advantage. So many others did without them, using only combinations of base expressions to describe everything. If he stopped to think about it, it saddened him. Eventually he worried that, if no one was interested in naming the innumerable things of the universe, or the endless permutations of human feeling that seemed to evolve along with the species, then humans would not be able to distinguish anything, and they would lose the capacity to feel intuitively. This, he concluded, mattered. In fact, it was all that mattered.

It was all that mattered now that Luke was old, now that most of his life was behind him. What was there left to name? There wasn't much time left, and there were gaping holes in his knowledge.

He began with rocks. He had been walking over them his whole life. He had driven through them, felt them under his toes at the beach, walked through buildings made of them. Rocks were made of earth. So was he. Statues were made of rock. Ruins, buried under layers of time, had been constructed lovingly of hewn rock. Rocks rained down from volcanoes and lifted from the soil in his garden. Pulverized, they could sink again through eons and return to rock.

Anthracite was a rock that once warmed his grandparents' homes. It filled Pittsburgh's skies with soot. Barges moved it up the Monongahela river to the mills, where it was burned to melt iron ore and produce steel. Steel from rocks. Steel to build skyscrapers, tanks, and bridges.

Every rock he picked up as a child contained streaks of other rocks. At school he learned that, after plants and animals died, they could turn into coal. But on the way down they became other rocks: organic sedimentary rocks, such as shale, siltstone, limestone, and dolostone. But these names only described traced of their purest forms, for they most often merged gradually into one another, along with rocks from the other two major categories—igneous and metamorphic. Minerals were born as rocks changed by pressure and heat. The earth's crust was nothing but ongoing rearrangement of forms.

Birds, too, could be identified by unique names. Redbirds, he found out, were actually cardinals. Sputzies were chipping sparrows, while bluebirds were not bluebirds at all, but blue jays. It seemed everything he knew from childhood had another name, one more commonly accepted outside the Pittsburgh suburban neighborhood of his upbringing, even if those original names had been told to him lovingly by a string of first-generation eastern and central European descendants.

From his woodland home Luke now lost his gaze in a hillside canopy of oaks, birches, maples, and dogwood. There he spied warblers, and was horrified to discover that there were dozens of different species of warbler, each with only the slightest distinction. Not only that, but many of them wore altered plumage while breeding, or as juveniles. It was maddening to identify them, but that's what he did.

Then there were the wrens, hawks, larks, vireos, and flycatchers. To say nothing of the sparrows. Had all these birds been flying above him, or hidden in the trees, his whole life? Had they passed by as he agonized over a chemistry exam, or lost sleep over a failed love? Might there be other worlds he was only dimly aware of then, such as the world of insects, the world of clouds, or the world of winds? What were all those clouds called, or those breezes, or grasshoppers? Things existed, without names, behind his back. But as soon as he called them by name he took part in their creation, because he could refer to them, either alone or with others, and they could then occupy not only their elusive niches, but human minds as well. In fact, the greater his catalogue of named objects, the less Luke was inclined to own things, because he knew their existence was not limited to a tactile state. The more his mental lists of birds, trees, rocks, clothing, furniture, bells, dogs, and horses grew, the more he could dream them up any time he wanted. Without maintenance.

Of course, with all this knowledge came impatience. Once a catalogue of whatever commenced, you inevitably expected it to be bottomless. Always more to know, more to discover. It was like being chained to a treadmill. *The wordless are happy,*[*] he once read. Perhaps words were making him unhappy and dissatisfied with himself. Was it time to shut the door on naming things?

He tried it. He stopped learning and began watching more television, or reviewing only that which he had already learned. There were 600 different species of oak tree. He knew them all. There exist nearly 22,000 species of ants. Those he hadn't mastered. Some things had to fall by the wayside.

He went to bed trying to empty his mind of all those picayune names: what worth had they, anyway? One could enjoy a magnolia warbler as well as a cerulean. One thing kept popping up though, no matter how hard he tried to keep it buried. That was his catalogue of faces.

The faces of his family and close friends held an obvious attraction; each of them inhabited the most intimate corners of his history. They contained whole ranges of emotions. Their elusiveness was not unlike the elusiveness of Luke's own life: so many states of being crammed into his soul that he could never come up with a complete definition of himself.

But then there were the others, an inexhaustible supply of faces he might have seen only once, but faces that carried deep representations of unique facets of humanity. Luke could not forget them. They resurfaced at the oddest times, and Luke never knew what they meant, those anonymous faces. But he could not dismiss them, for they filled little voids in the puzzle of existence.

In some way, then, they comforted him in the way a mother's hug or child's hand or lovemaking episode couldn't.

---

* Virginia Woolf, in her diary.

What was most exciting about this was that he knew there would always be more, everywhere, all the time. He would never know them all, yet he knew he could count on numbers of them to add to this intriguing, unpredictable catalogue.

It struck Luke that he didn't know himself. It struck him many times during his life. He knew this because whenever he envisioned himself doing anything, the face he envisioned was not his. It would most often be the face of a stranger or acquaintance he might have met only once. It didn't matter what gender they were, or how old, or when they had lived (historical characters appeared as well). What mattered was the aspect of Luke they represented.

Luke the accomplished artist? That was a colleague he'd met at a conference, the one whose work Luke had always admired. Luke the courageous and outspoken? That was Winston Churchill, or the nurse who had taken care of him as a child at St. Joseph's Hospital. Luke the withdrawn and confused? That was the scientist from China Leah had brought home for dinner, the faraway look in her eyes as she sat down to eat. And the many Lukes of the future? Why, they were everywhere: silver-haired gentlemen reading the newspaper on the subway, Walt Whitman with a long white beard, a great-grandmother with well-lived circles under her eyes, a boy whose eyes flashed the way Luke's did—his great, great grandson. Luke would become all of them; they flashed like beacons in the distance.

What did adults mean when they spoke of love? He loved his mother, but he also loved blooming cherry trees and mud (because that's where salamanders lived).

Sometimes he just loved. On good days he loved everything, so he thought love must mean having a good day. But even on bad days he could find something to love, even if it was a worm on the sidewalk. Love must mean finding surprises.

Love could lead him down strange paths. He loved books. Each one was an adventure, a place where he could no longer feel his own body, or know that he was hungry or tired. He loved each of the worlds books created. It didn't matter how he felt about them, whether he liked the story or not. What mattered was the magic. That was love too.

As an adolescent love became even more confusing. He became more aware of his love for experiences, evenings he spent with his friends, hellos in the school corridors, solidarity in the unified battle against teachers and anything institutional.

In art class he fell in love with human bodies: hard muscular ones and soft curvy ones. They drew models whose forms were strange and new to him, from a rather skinny, mouse-faced woman whose ribs he could see beneath her skin to a woman eight months pregnant to a bearded man who appeared to be made of sticks.

Outside of class he began to notice the variety of the human form, and he could be attracted to any he found interesting. Most often it was manifested by the pom-pom girls, but it also showed up in the long stride of a distance runner on his track team, a wrestler he didn't know too well but whose locker was next to his, and most importantly, in iconic women of the past such as Greta Garbo, Rita Hayworth, and Marilyn Monroe. He found photographs of them in magazines which he tucked in his desk drawers beneath doodle-covered notebooks and old homework assignments. Late at night he would pull them out and peer at them, trying to understand how anything so beautiful could have ever walked the earth.

He, too, could be beautiful, if beauty was enigma. Every evening he stared at himself in the mirror; he had become so different from the asthmatic, cow-licked child he had once seen there. The new Luke had begun to resemble relatives he had seen in those sepia-tinted photographs, relatives long gone whose lives he knew next to nothing about. Now he knew next to nothing about himself.

What could he do? Inhabiting a newly transformed body, unsure of his instincts, unsure of the future, and unsure that he would ever find someone to wrap soft arms around him to shield him from all this uncertainty, he tended to himself as if he were a rare species in danger of extinction. He maintained a fit body through exercise (mostly with the track team), ate heartily but wisely, groomed his hair meticulously, and took care in selecting clothes that seemed to reflect what he felt inside. In this way he could present himself to a soul mate more completely, should that day ever come.

By and by he did find someone, and for a while love was as easy as pie. There was nothing unpredictable and insane about it; it only made him smile all day long. Chilly fall evenings he walked with her hand-in-hand, smelling her hair and tasting her lips when they kissed. Jeez, nothing had ever been so good. All of his life's misfortunes dulled or disappeared. This was part of a new world order, a brave beginning, a dazzling light. And then, just as he was about to settle in to a long and happy life with her, she dumped him for a senior.

They were fifteen years old.

All the lights were extinguished, leaving Luke to lie awake in a shadow-filled bedroom, unable to come to any conclusion. He went to classes with black rings beneath his eyes, wore colorless clothes, and lost his trademark: a wide smile.

The school year came to an end, and he spent the summer running, working, reading, painting—anything but pointless hanging around. That was what the two of them had done together: existed, merely, with no ulterior motive other than to be in each other's company. She had proven that wrong.

Come September he began a new school year, taking only the hardest classes, remaining loyal to friends but imbued with a new seriousness, a realization that his life would only be as good as that which he worked for. Even love, he decided, would not come free.

And yet, he continued to find that he loved everywhere. Glimpses of that dazzling light seemed to call his attention: it was in his little brother's hair, in scarlet alongside Prussian blue on his palette, in the hillside of leafless trees, in his grandmother's Christmas cookies, in a multiple choice test whose material he had mastered. He slowly became aware that love was not an all-or-nothing affair. It had nooks and crannies all over existence. Its brightness could sustain you, not merely overwhelm you.

When he finally met up with Leah again he had been nurturing this appreciation for omnipresent love, and yet he felt with her that he was being transported back in time to the overwhelming kind. This, however, was not a bad thing, because he welcomed it now on more solid ground. He knew it was an illusion that must pass, but he was also sure that it made him more human to accept it. He even felt that self-confidence that comes from pointed love returning. He was a bit older now, and he had suffered trials and tribulations well beyond those of high school. Leah's love gave him a much needed break, an infusion of feeling that channeled all that anonymous, worldly love into one, tangible human being again.

Along came Ivan. Uh-oh. Another funnel for love. Was love divisible? Luke felt his love for Ivan growing, and his love for Leah growing old. Strangely, this didn't bother him. For he could still say he loved her. Was love transforming again? If so, it was not something to mourn, but celebrate. It meant love was expanding from within him. Love would flow out from him now as much as it had flowed in during the past. And Leah was almost solely responsible for letting that happen.

Luke, warm in his bed, feeling the slight twinge of his asthma but drifting off nonetheless, believed God and Mary and Saint Blaise were all glowing above him. He felt the glow of his father and Aunt Celine there too. He knew they would be there during all the cold hours of the night, along with Santa Claus and a few others like Louise who used to live upstairs in what was now his bedroom, and Abraham Lincoln. This glowing was something better than light. It was light and warmth and a good empty feeling all put together. The empty feeling was good because it let them have a place inside him. They made him feel safe inside there, like being in a big room full of blankets when snow was falling outside.

Luke was not particularly concerned about turning thirty, nor forty. He had always been able to think ahead and prepare himself for the future decades of his life. He did this by observing others in those age brackets, and by putting himself in their shoes. But things were a little different by the time he reached his fifties. By then he had become outspoken.

Not that he had never before shared an opinion, but usually those opinions were either somewhat timid or vociferous to the point of being suspect, as if he were trying to convince himself. He had almost always approached a formal setting with his heart in his throat, and could rarely defend anything that grew from an institution, be it church, government, family, or doctors. In fact, his brain almost always worked in the opposite direction: cleverly finding ways to undermine any assumption people made about time-honored modes of thinking and behavior. But, being in his fifties, well, most probably marked a half-way point in his life. Perhaps he was even already passed it. In any case, the rest would inevitably be downhill. No time to dilly-dally.

With this new position came equanimity. Nothing really frightened him, least of all authority and mysterious organizations. They were all, he'd finally come to realize, frauds. Most of them took advantage of misinformed, frightened people who had been brainwashed into thinking that they must always be stuck in a certain level of "intelligence," compliance, or society. Luke had had a feeling all along that this wasn't true, and now he was sure of it. All you had to do to change yourself, or the way others saw you, was speak up. There were no levels, only degrees of self-confidence.

Looking back, Luke deleted all the useless worrying he had done about his future. How well would he do in school? What kind of job would he have? Which shoes to buy? Whom to marry? These had been verifiable preoccupations, but in retrospect each of them seemed trivial next to the new course his life would be taking, namely, the way of compassion, conscience, and spontaneity. Nothing he would do belonged to the future, only the present. He would sleep well every night, knowing he had kept to this path.

Now the funny thing was that, when Luke interacted with others, be they at work, Ivan's school, or the world of commerce, his new attitude seemed to be infectious. A dose of unaffected honesty was what everyone craved. And for those holdouts who insisted on continuing on the road of lies, posturing, and deception, Luke was able to mow them down simply and elegantly. Their stubbornness became their own undoing, welling up inside them and choking them as they went home to ponder this outspoken guy who challenged their most cherished delusions.

Life was no longer about working toward some end, then. It was about preparing for the end. He realized that this end was always around the corner, that it had always been that way. Why had it taken him fifty years to believe it?

School was easy and fun and full of colors, but the kids on the upper floors were scary. They lugged around big books. They talked too much; and they made a lot of noise tramping up and down the stairs. Upstairs was a mystery, a place he would eventually find himself in. How would he be able to do it? Even the teachers up there were scary, their eyes always moving and mouths ready to bark out orders.

The older kids studied subjects with confusing names like algebra and literature. They were closer to the top of the long ladder he and everyone else must climb. At the very top of the ladder sat college, an unimaginable place of torture and sadness where kids turned into adults. Some people, like his mother and grandparents, never went to college, so they became adults by getting married. The ones who didn't go to college were a little happier than the ones who did. His doctor, who had been to college, always seemed angry.

Now when he grew up and became an adult he would no longer be just Luke, he would have to be something else too. A doctor. A teacher. A pilot. This was something exciting to look forward to, but it was also a little confusing and even sad. Why couldn't he be just Luke? He liked being Luke. He never wanted to be anyone else. Being a pilot would be fun, but then he would still come home to eat dinner and love people, and find ladybugs in the garden. That was not being a pilot. Why then were adults always asking him what he wanted to be? He wanted to be Luke!

His idea of Luke-ness spread far and wide, the older he got. He left parts of Luke in every place he visited, in every thought he thought, in every person he met. There was no hope of drawing them back in to snuggle together to be the childhood Luke he had been. By then he knew that he could only become what he already was: a being self-contained whose will allowed him to live most of his life outside of himself. It had nothing to do with attainments, and everything to do with how he transported himself, and the impressions he found along the way.

After working several years as a graphic artist he began to see everything he'd created—logos, posters, brochures—piled up around him inside his brain, and they began to suffocate him. When new clients came to see him he would show them his portfolio, and for a while he thought he was showing them things inside him.

But that was not the case. What he was showing them was small slivers of time, each one polished for its own selfish end. But together they represented nothing that Luke recognized as himself. That Luke was still wonderfully elusive and whole, invisible, but more present and solid than anything he had created. It would be the only thing worth knowing when he died.

At school there were no uniforms, neither for boys nor girls, as there were rumored to be at other schools. It didn't matter what you wore, you were all treated the same. You waited in straight lines, standing on the green floor tiles, for your turn in the lavatory. You all learned to write the same way, read from the same books, sing the same songs in church. And even when you were angry and felt out of step, you didn't feel you were alone. It was as if you were spread around in everybody. You couldn't hide.

Years later, when Luke sometimes felt that he didn't know who he was, or where he belonged, he still felt that he was somewhat protected, that he was still spread around, and would mysteriously come out okay.

So now he is wondering, sitting in front of his window on the natural world, what has been natural in his life, and what has been forced. How much of it was merely passing seconds on the clock; how much of it consumed by a wider, more in-clusive time? He considered the things he remembered most, how they crowded out those clock-seconds and welled up like mighty waves inside him. Most of those waves had been made by those he'd loved, ripples that swelled slowly over the years, leaving the anonymous sea in their wake.

What was in that anonymous sea? What depths did it reach? What secrets did it hold? Luke could never know, because it was filled with voided, anonymous seconds, all those he'd lived and disregarded. It was a sea of confusion, of discouragement and cowardice. Everything he had decided against, including the voices of those who professed doom and gloom.

But the tidal wave rolled over all the days of his life, holding him above the chaos of the sea like his mother's arms, as well as the arms of everyone who had given him hope along the way. It took him for quite a ride, obliterating all the despair below. For all the material world was liquid, while the actions and words of people were solid and enduring, lifting him ever higher and affording him a clear view. Without them, he would have long ago died of loneliness and defeat.

She met him in Limerick, Ireland one early morning in September. He had come to meet her there following three months in Eastern Europe. Shannon airport was not crowded that day, another nice day in a string of sunny days that everyone said was unusual for Ireland.

She did seem tall to him—was that something he had forgotten about her? Her hair was a bit more curly now, the current fashion. But her eyes were the same, bright and welcoming to Luke, who hadn't seen her in so many years.

They spent that day touring the town, poking their heads through stone arches in an old castle, walking with hands intertwined down a cobblestone street along the River Shannon. After a few hours it was as if they had never been separated. Laughter returned to them; spontaneity guided them through a time that existed only for them.

For the next few days they rented a car and roamed the west of Ireland. They followed the coastlines of Connemara and Galway, passing nothing but peat bogs, sheep, and a stillness that uncovered their souls, so that they were bare in each other's presence.

At one point the road ascended a small hill where wild fuchsia grew in thick bushes. They slowed to admire the view of the low-lying fields and distant sea. Just below them lay a small graveyard, abandoned it seemed, and enclosed by a wrought iron fence. They couldn't help wanting to have a closer look at its magnificent old tombstones.

While inside the gated yard a wind rose up from the lowlands and curled around the few trees, tall stones, and them. Luke began telling Leah about a dream he'd had several months ago while still in California. He had dreamt of his father, a rare occurrence, one that he could not remember happening before. In the dream his father stared at Luke and said nothing. Luke could see him very clearly again while inside that graveyard with Leah. He tried explaining it to her, looking away, but then she touched him and released from him a flood of tears. She held him so close he could feel her heart beating. *Oh Luke!* she said. *I know! I know!*

Fire and Ice

A novella

by

MARK SABA

TOM

On the way to school I keep to the familiar—the familiar alleyways and side streets, the familiar ups and downs of hills, the homes whose colors I have memorized, the gas station, the fire house. My feet have gotten used to the early morning rhythm; they know exactly how many steps it will take to get to the last hill, where my orange-brick school building looms.

Once it was scary, a foreign country where everything was surprisingly and terrifyingly in order. I was to become part of that order. I had no say in it. So I welcomed the order, though inside I knew I was still free. I learned that school was a game everyone needed to play. All you had to do was take in something and then give it back. It would take twelve years of taking in things, then you went on to college, and God knows what went on there. By that time you would be an adult, and the game would be over. But adults seemed to have a game too.

All of life (and the preparations necessary for death) is confined to my school. We are constantly reminded of a man who lived two thousand years ago. The stories about that man are almost always about miracles, and as long as there are miracles there is nothing in life that we can not conquer.

Because life has to be organized, so too are the classrooms where we learn about it. Our books, pencils, and crayons must be neatly tucked away under our desktops. When the nuns hand out other books or mimeographed sheets they seem to appear from nowhere. And after we have finished with them they return to their mysterious hiding places. If we create anything with our popsicle sticks, construction paper, and sweet-smelling glue, the artwork either hangs briefly in perfect rows on the bulletin boards or sits on the window sills before we take it home.

The nuns, though they are different people, all dress the same. That way we know who they are not because of what they wear but by what they say and how they act. And some of them wear glasses. The other teachers look more like our mothers and dress differently, but somehow they are all the same too. They are calm and always know which direction we are going in, the same direction that's in our books.

As long as we can go from point A to point B, and then to C, D, and all the way down the road to Z (which will be sometime in twelfth grade) we will be fine. And after that we will go to college to learn how to be adults, one book at a time. It's nice to know where you are headed.

ANNE

I see school buildings sometimes when we are driving, my mother and I, to the supermarket or the gas station. I see kids hanging around the doorways, pouring out of busses, waking in twos and threes. I love my teacher, my mother. She almost always answers my questions, and when she can't, I can usually find answers with my grandfather, who likes to give me an answer that contains another question. This makes me figure out answers myself. Learning is about questions and figuring stuff out, usually with more questions.

During the winter I read a lot of books. I draw and cook and paint. We have more time for lessons, and my mother and

I speak in French. Early spring is my favorite time of year. It's when we begin preparing the flats for seeds. It's when I begin smelling the earth again, when the sun gently strokes everything back to life. I hear the little frogs peeping in the vernal ponds and the robins chasing one another around the yards. I study each type of seedling and compare them to my botany book. I find out where they come from, what part of the world, and how we've changed them from their original ancestors. That gets me interested in geography, and history, and I begin asking my grandfather about his European ancestors. When he tells stories I never forget them. There is no need to repeat them over and over in my head in order to memorize them. They are just there, forever.

Each year I watch the seeds grow, and each year I am surprised by them, by how sturdy and fearless they are. I never know what world I am stepping into when I greet them in the morning. I see epic novels there, civilizations rising, graveyards overrun by new births. It's very exciting because I feel I am part of it. I feed, water, and monitor whole worlds.

TOM

We pray every morning, always with Special Intentions read over the loudspeaker by Sister Mary Grace. That way we can all pray for the same thing. Then we add our own prayers silently at the end. When you pray, you think about something or someone and that's the only thing you are thinking about. If every one thinks about it together for a long time a miracle can happen. It's because of the prayers.

In church we sit, stand, and kneel, also together. We might be thinking about different things but we are all doing the same things and saying the same things—other kinds of prayers. Those prayers are mostly old-fashioned and don't make sense to me. But they sound nice when we say them together. We sing prayers too, and I have my favorites of those.

Church is quiet. It is quiet even when people are praying. The pews and windows are quiet. The crucifix is quiet. So are the altar boys and the statues near the altar. Sometimes I don't like going there, but once I am inside I feel very nice. I feel that no one can hurt me, and I feel I have nothing to do but sit, stand, kneel, and pray. It's an easy thing to do, and no one is going to grade you on it.

ANNE

We don't talk about God much and when we do we treat him just like one of us, as if he were in the same room, or walking along the fields as we go to look for blueberries. If I ask my mother about him, she is never afraid to explain him to me, and when I don't understand she doesn't become upset, only listens.

I feel God today, I sometimes say. I say it when there is no other way to describe what I'm feeling, like when I'm watching birds fight, or when I'm sitting alone in a room after Aunt Emily died. Why does God make people die? Because, my mother says, we are part of a cycle, a cycle we don't really understand, but we see hints of it around us every day. We must never think we are above, or better than, the cycle. We have to trust that it is, all in all, a good thing. I do not look convinced. And she says, no one is convinced, but we can comfort one another to build that trust. Togetherness. That's the word she uses.

That must be it. Why I have eyes. To see the cycle, to think about it. To see someone else, to connect to that person. My eyes make me think.

TOM

There is a way to do everything. I don't know them all yet, but I'm sure they are there. Like the way to make pancakes, the way to get dressed in the morning, the way to say hello to adults, and the way to take down a Christmas tree. It never matters that I don't know how to do something, because all I have to do is ask and I'll find out. Lots of things you can find out how to do from books, and lots of things you can find out from people. Especially grandparents. They have spent their whole lives already learning how to do everything, so they might as well just tell you and save you the trouble.

If you know how to cook a turkey you don't ever need to change it. Just always cook it that way. Then spend your time learning how to do other things. By the time you're a grandparent you'll know just about everything.

ANNE

This morning I took a long walk down to the store to buy bubble gum. My mother doesn't care if I chew it but she will not buy it for me. I have to use my allowance. At first it was chilly but then I warmed up from walking, and by the time I came back I felt hot. I threw my jacket on the ground and walked over to check on my guinea pigs in the cage my dad made for them. The female, Jill, was pregnant and I wasn't sure how long it would take for the babies to grow inside her.

I opened the lid of the cage and out came Jill from the nesting box I had put in there. She was all skinny! Then Jack followed, and both of them were chattering away, glad to see me. My heart jumped as I lifted the lid of the box to see the babies. And they were there, but they were all dead. My uncle, who is a farmer and knows a lot about animals, said I shouldn't have let Jack stay in the cage with a pregnant female. He said Jack probably killed the babies. I wanted to know why, as that didn't make sense to me. He said that's the way nature was, it didn't always make sense to us. From then on I raised tropical fish instead, but I soon found out that fish eat their babies too. When I went to the zoo I asked the man who fed the monkeys if they ate their babies, and he laughed. I don't know why it was funny.

I asked my mother this question too: if she was starving, would she eat her baby? She told me some people have eaten dead people in special circumstances, and sometimes even not in special circumstances. She said it wasn't for us to judge. I said I didn't want to judge, but it was making me sick. Then I went for a walk, and noticed that everything outside was eating one another. I wasn't feeling sick though; I just watched the birds catching insects and spiders sucking the life out of flies and beetles carrying off little chunks of a dead raccoon and my cat Oscar going after a chipmunk. It all seemed normal to me, even if I didn't like it.

TOM

I grew up and went off into the world, not knowing who I was, or where I would go. I brought with me only everything I had seen, heard, and felt up to that point. My senses had been honed into a prism, and that prism was what made me.

Who am I? I've traveled enough to know that I see myself differently under different kinds of weather, stuck into various bits of scenery. Even those who call my name affect the feeling I have for myself. Yet I have a distinct sense of being, and of somehow taking part in the creation of my being.

In the course of that creation I have been pulled in many directions. Why am I not torn to pieces? I've found myself content to wander, confronting unpleasantries and comforts with the same skin. If the universe is unfolding, then so am I. There is, and never has been, a blueprint. And yet I've seen whole nations strive to live by them. Whole systems, whole traditions, whole packages of condescension and arrogance. I can only observe. My only solace is that I know, deep down, everyone shares my dilemma. This is what allows us to connect.

In my neighborhood all the yards are attractive. Each spring we rake them clean, till the gardens, plant flowers and vegetables, and take evening walks to size them up. Gardening is an endless battle. We battle bugs, storms, drought, and seasons out of sync. You can't let a garden go for very long, because nature is at it 24–7 trying to dismantle everything you've done. Nature doesn't like that we've planted our houses in even rows right in her random domain. She might want certain trees to come down, and others to flourish. You may not agree with her.

Twenty-five years ago, when I was still married, I planted a lilac bush. It didn't do well in the spot I had chosen—behind the garage—so after a couple of years I moved it out into more sunlight. Lilacs, I learned, have more blooms if you deadhead the previous year's, and even then they seem to be on a two-year cycle.

The lilac grew, but so did my job, my waistline, and everything else in the yard. Everything required my care, and the lilac seemed to carry on without me. I noticed that its leaves turned a powdery white in summer, and many dropped off, and by autumn they turned an unattractive brown. But by winter its stems were clean and ready to hibernate new buds for spring.

Occasionally I trimmed it, especially the branches that leaned so far to one side I thought the whole bush would fall over. After a round of particularly heavy snowfalls one year I noticed the bush was particularly deranged. I'm not sure anyone noticed but I had to chop it back to some semblance of uprightness. I couldn't let it face the world as it was, lopsided and unsure of itself. So at twenty-five it looks again like it did when I first bought it, trim and spare, and still in the business of setting new buds. Who knows how it might have fared it I hadn't kept at least one eye on it all that time. After all, it was our first child in this house, a symbol of the hope we had for our success there. It would be a sin to let symbols go to waste, the way of nature. I'm thinking that lilac bush will outlive the family we had once planned to have. It will whisper love, and hope, to the strangers who inherit this house, even if they will not hear it.

ANNE

The night the storm came we tucked ourselves into bed and listened to the wailing wind. I sat up once to peek out the window, and it was nothing but silvery darkness on the other side. We awakened to over three feet of snow, our impassable street, and two once-towering pines lying cross-wise in our backyard, one of them having demolished our garage. It took three weeks to have them removed, and even longer to have the garage repaired. During that time my mother fell ill with pneumonia. I drove through ice and snow to visit her at the hospital daily. Sometimes we just sat and said nothing as I flipped through magazines and she adjusted the throw I had brought to cover her legs.

That winter was different. I was not bothered by the cold, nor the snow, nor our yard in ruins. I had come to believe that life was that way—a series of ruins we must deal with—and that made everything in my life seem to fall into place. Even the years I had questioned suffering, or anything outside of my control.

There was my mother, my teacher and life-long guardian, reduced to a task I had acquired. I had to think of how to keep her nourished, clean, and warm, just as I had once tended our greenhouse seedlings. I began to see her as part of the cycle, the incomprehensible plan of our spinning Earth to devour its own creations, again and again, in its intricate and hostile ways. I could allay the hostility, but ultimately I would fail to keep my mother here, stuck in her own cycle, the cycle that must finish, just as the cycle had finished for my father years ago.

During those days I attended her funeral many times in my mind. I imagined all the people connected to her life pouring in to pay tribute, then disappear onto their own lonely paths. What more could I do? I comforted myself by knowing what must happen, and I wanted to thank my mother for having prepared me to accept it. Yet I couldn't, because she was no longer that mother. I could say the words but I wasn't sure she would hear them, understand them, or be able to respond to them.

It's funny, knowing you are on your own, finally, even though you've mentally prepared for it for as along as you can remember. I felt I was walking on air, nothing to support me.

TOM

The house I live in has been around. I've taken it across oceans, arranged it carefully according to my circumstances, loaded it with objects lovingly placed, worn comfort into its furniture and dishes. You could say a house has transformative power: it defines as much as it is defined. It is laden with ghosts, the sum of the daily ghosts of those who have chosen it as a place to live.

It's important to take care of those ghosts. They are a house's soul. If you neglect them, or forfeit them to wandering, you may be putting your soul in jeopardy as well. Because a wandering soul has no boundaries, nothing to place it within the framework of a life. And what makes a life are all the things it attaches to along the way; things to dream about and put into order, in a house.

The house I grew up in is the one I've been taking with me wherever I go. If I'm lying on the couch in mid-afternoon with eyes closed my heart jumps as I reconsider where I am. Do the stairs run up the center of the house, between living and dining rooms, opposite the front door? Or do they hug the far wall? Is the kitchen in the back of the house? How do I get down to the basement? Coat closet? I don't know where I am, or what I I'm feeling. Memory? Desire? Remorse? Or do I wish for nothing but my childhood?

ANNE

I don't like being inside. Even in winter I'll take long walks, happy to make my way among the snow banks and fallen tree limbs. When I re-enter the house I bring the wilderness with me. My heart has been opened and I feel up to any task. Although one task I have never been up to is cleaning the house.

When I think of my house, or any house, I think of dust. Where on Earth does it all come from? Something wants to defile a house, send layer upon layer of filth into it to cover up anything you've put there. Outside, we see it happen more obviously. But there it doesn't seem to bother us, because we don't really need to direct it. Nature will take care of itself, no matter how unseemly from our selfish point of view. Houses are untamed pets, always seeking out some new kind of naughty behavior to make you shake your head and sometimes lead you to despair.

It began snowing as I made my way home from my morning walk that day. I like the time leading up to a snow: the still birds and trees, the sky one indeterminate color, the way sound carries under it. I had seen big snowfalls before, but I had no idea this snowfall would be historical.

I awoke the next day to forty inches of it. When I first looked out the window I saw nothing but undulating white waves, perfectly coiffed. No creature had marked them with footprints; no stray leaves or twigs marred their unique perfection. I was awestruck. It took another hour before I had the nerve to go out to start shoveling, and even then the experience thrilled me from head to toe. I didn't care about the sagging roof and fallen gutters, nor my car held hostage inside the garage, nor the power outage, the cold. I felt gifted, pleasantly powerless, at peace. If, as they say, these super-storms will persist, I may find myself reveling in them.

TOM

A strange couple has moved into my neighborhood. I'm not sure they are a couple at all. They are two women: one dark-haired and portly, the other tall and bird-like, with sandy blond hair that continually brushes her forehead. Seems like every time I want to introduce myself to them, they disappear.

They must be professionals. Their lifestyle is clean and well-heeled, but not ostentatious. Still, I wish they were a little more vigilant about their yard. One minute it is overgrown and spotty, the next it is newly planted with expensive annuals. The house itself is maintained, even if it is painted some odd shade of gray/violet/rose that I can never put my finger on while it changes with the light. Occasionally a black limousine pulls up and whisks either one or both of them away. Then someone will stop by their house in the evening. They must have pets in there.

Anyway, these women went knocking on my door one fine spring day to announce their initiative in natural disaster planning. Yes, on a heaven-sent, perfect day in May they wanted to touch base about hurricanes, epic snowfalls, and crashing trees. I said no thanks, I'd rather tend to my garden. They said some day there might not be a garden for me to tend. I thought for a moment and replied: I can always build a sunroom, climate-controlled. For some reason they were shaking their heads, but smiling. I wished them well and sent them on their way. I wondered, after they left, about people who had time for such crusades. How does that work?

ANNE

Funny, I often forget how old I am. I feel I've been alive forever. I live where I am, not in something I've constructed. My
memories reside independently of the place where I perceived
them; objects merely acted as props in the play. So I am at
home anywhere, any time, as long as I'm a part of this planet.

Everything I know is tied to our little farm. That is where
I learned about death, about rebirth, about just about anything there was. If I didn't see it first-hand I heard it from my
mother's mouth, or from the books she chose for me to read.
We solved problems together—abstract algebraic problems as
well as ethical problems, problems as old as humankind. The
only order I knew was the cycle of day and night, of hunger
and fulfillment, of the seasons eternally bleeding into one another.

I awoke each morning knowing exactly what was needed
for that day. If it was a day in February I measured out the
sphagnum moss in which to plant perennial seeds. If it was a
day in November I might dig up the leeks. In July I followed
dragonflies and birch beetles. In January I read Emerson or
listened to Stravinsky. Rarely did we buy anything that was
not needed to sustain us. I had my winter boots and summer
sandals, three pairs of shorts and five or six dresses for any
special occasion. The rest was a blur.

And that is why, after our house became a partial heap of charred rubble, I found it easy to live in the tool shed my father and grandfather had built.

The meteor came crashing though the roof as I slept, as if a train had run through the house and then disappeared out the other side. Before I could gather my wits I was overcome by a smell that made me wonder if I'd left a kettle to boil out on the stove all night. I had heard of tornadoes that sound like freight trains, or trees that came crashing through a window on a windy night. But this night was calm and clear. I wondered how loud things could get in dreams.

But the burning smell brought me quickly to my senses. I got out of bed and put on my slippers. By then I saw fire coming up the stairs, so I fled the house by climbing out a back window, which led me to a porch roof. From there I leapt to the ground, and watched part of my house go up in flames as the fire trucks arrived.

The shed does me fine most of the time. My wits keep me company there, and I am able to ride out storms, heat waves, and frigid cold snaps as long as I prepare for them. Most of the time it's just living though, and now that it's become so simple, it seems I am living longer, as if time has actually spread itself thinner.

TOM

My life has been divided not by days but by relationships—relationships I've had with others who helped define those divisions. If I had been brought into this world as a wildman living alone in a cave I doubt I would remember much of it in the end. What is an endless succession of miserable days tacked onto an endless cycle of seasons? It's too much like infinity, or death.

Sometimes I imagine cities as they were in the distant past, even before they were built, when they were little more than rearranged dirt and landscaped plots. Who then determined what they would one day become? How was their fate coordinated, by what rules? A hallowed monument, commemorating the deaths of those who died defending a society, is built on the same ground that buries the sewage lines. A stately apartment building facing a breathtaking marine view shares a hillside with crows that devour a blue jay's young. The college student who studies days on end for a final exam passes the cleaning lady in his dorm who is having a good day because she has its predictable order tucked away in her head.

I imagine also cities that have yet to be built: wooded hillsides and marshy estuaries where infinite, tiny lives flourish and are ruined before we clear away their remains to build fortresses of human ingenuity, fortresses that allow our peculiar emotions to play out with little regard to the laws of nature. If I could, I'd like to watch history play out from a particular vantage point. I would see a city's evolution like a great, multi-faceted organism containing multitudes of symbiotic creatures, a complexity that we alone have engendered. And within that city, that visible organism, lie our ideas and imaginations, both of which lead to ever more complexity in the way we build things and govern ourselves: the fruit we call miracles.

ANNE

I met a curious man this morning at the neighborhood store where I sell my vegetables. As I was unloading my crates of broccoli he asked if I was having a good year. At first I thought it strange that someone I didn't know should inquire into my personal life. Then I realized he was talking about my income (I think) from selling vegetables. I replied, I guess so. As long as there is sun and rain I'm fine. He chuckled.

And what about what you bring to the table?

Anyone can do what I do. All it takes is a little experience. The rest is common sense.

He looked perplexed. But I wanted to get back home in time for the storm, so I didn't pursue the conversation. We parted politely.

Storms are so lovely from where I watch them, on the little porch attached to my shed. I get wet, and once or twice I think the lightning was at my back, but that only makes it more worthwhile. What else is there to do in violent weather, but study it? A good storm hits all my senses: I smell it as soon as it arrives; it lodges in my bones; I am knocked breathless by great swaths of blues and grays, and even the trees change color. The pelting rain creates melody out of chaos, and peels of thunder make my blood roar.

Sometimes I choose something to read during a storm. It's not that I will find the same emotions in a book that I feel from the weather, but whatever the book is telling me, it will sink in more deeply. Reading, for me, is an exercise in humility. The book and I approach each another with open arms, but soon I am settled in its bosom, letting it soothe me with its wisdom. There is no other way for me to try to understand why I am here, or how I should interact with others who find themselves in the same conundrum of existence. If a book fails me, it is because it has no art, no refinement in it message. In that case it is little more than an amusement park ride, and I have little use for amusement parks. There is plenty about me every day to provide amusement.

TOM

I am fascinated by numbers: how they measure everything, the way they level out the playing field. You can't argue with them. You can use them as weapons, or as a method of peaceful persuasion. They can be the only unbiased source of comfort or despair. Maybe that's why I am an accountant.

I wear a bracelet that tells me how many calories I burn every day, how many steps I've taken, how fast my heart is beating, and how many pounds I've lifted. It frees me to think about other things, then tally up the state of my health at the end of a day. Truly miraculous.

I like to spend free time reading charts and graphs. They help me navigate and make sense of this world. I like knowing how many beans it would take, end-to-end, to reach the moon, for instance; or how many Tiffanys there are in Los Angeles. I also want to know what percent of Great Lakes Catholics voted for our current president, and what percent have had an abortion.

Statistics connect us all. It doesn't matter what religion you are, or who your parents were, or where you went to school. If I feel like a number, it's only because I am, and that number will help me get social security benefits, a driver's license, a discount at the drug store, a way to store my money in the bank, even a win for my soccer team.

Lately we've all been a bit worried about climate change, but I believe numbers, through science, will save us in the end. We will be able to calculate the rate of the rising sea level, and know in advance which cities are therefore most at risk. We will use better computers to generate probabilities to track storms, and parcel out supplies according to populations. Everything will be counted and recounted. We will beat nature once again by recycling our "waste" and turning it into alternate items. No more masses of unaccounted for goods; everything will be accounted for according to ever-more accurate metrics.

This is the world we live in, the one we created, and will tend to, as long as we go on recreating it.

ANNE

I don't really understand why people like to travel—to wait in lines at airports and train stations, to put up with digestive failure, unfamiliar bugs, and exasperated foreigners who throw up their hands at you and appear to be rude. I traveled a bit when I was younger. But now I see the folly in traveling for pleasure. My most rewarding trips have been the educational ones, the ones I took off-season, when I saw people as they truly are, and they looked upon me as an equal, in their daily lives.

I welcome visitors to my home, even strangers. After all, I don't have much to steal. I enjoy their company; they are as good as books. I like people who become part of my daily life, not players in outlandish events like weddings, or props in orchestrates scenes as those we see when "on vacation."

One of my friends, Walt, collects junk. He lives a short distance down the road. His property bleeds seamlessly into the surrounding countryside, and he tends the wild as much as his somewhat tamed grounds. Once Walt had come to me looking to borrow a casserole dish. I had one, and I lent it to him. On his way out the door he bumped into another friend of mine, Helen, who rarely visits me anymore. She took one look at him and ran. What was it about Walt that made her do that? Walt and I had a good laugh about it, but I could tell underneath he was a little spooked by the experience. I mean, Walt wouldn't hurt a turtle. All I could think of was the way he looked. Not his appearance. The way he *looked*. There is something underneath Walt that, I think, might scare people. It's in his eyes. They are not evil eyes, or intimidating, or even penetrating eyes. They are, purely and simply, honest—so full of honesty that people don't know quite how to handle them. Maybe they've never seen honesty before, and the physical evidence of it is too unnerving.

Something else about Walt: he is hard to locate in time. There is nothing about his clothing that would give it away. He might even be a ghost transported here from the 1870s, 1930s, or 1970s. I don't even have a clue how old he is. But this thing about Walt that scares people away—I think I am drawn to it. He is, in some way, a reflection of my own life. I'm not growing an economy. Neither am I intent on knocking down everyone else as competitors. It does no good, and besides, I don't get it. I'm more interested in tending to the planet in my small, interconnected way. When I go, I'll go in peace.

TOM

My yard is never the same from year to year. One year blight gets the tomatoes, the next they are as perfect and abundant as the crabgrass. One year the lilac overflows with heady blooms, the next I can barely find a few rusting before they have even opened every bud. Some blame this vegetative insanity on climate change. Others, like me, just go along with it and do what I can do to correct it.

I've started a neighborhood collective called StopWatch to deal with nature's vagaries. We pool our resources in these uncertain times: helping to shovel one another out under four feet of snow, trading gardening secrets, sharing ice and food stores when the electricity grid fails. I'm confident we can survive anything if we do it together.

Now my lady friends a few doors away are often enthusiastic about this initiative, so much that they can seem to be a bit over-zealous. That crazy winter, a couple of days before a major storm was supposed to hit, they took it upon themselves to traverse the neighborhood with a push-basket to collect canned goods, which they then intended to distribute after the ensuing melee. But the storm never quite came. It skirted us to the north, and we were left wondering what had become of our stock provisions. But the couple didn't come around again. I think they had left for Machu Picchu, and upon returning, seemed to have forgotten all about it. Another neighbor told me she had bumped into them at the grocery store and reported that they had planned to keep the provisions for the next bad weather event. I thought that a bit presumptuous. But what could we do?

ANNE

The past few days have given us remarkable sunsets, unlike any I have ever seen. The red is nearly crimson, a wide swath of it every evening that barely fades, but is eclipsed by darkness.

I don't read the news much, and don't own a TV, but people at the market are talking. It seems a pretty big volcano has blown its top off somewhere in south Asia, and its ashes are causing those sunsets here, halfway around the globe. And the thing is still spewing, so I guess I'll be entertained every evening for some time. I wonder if I should be hanging out my wash. I don't own a dryer either.

TOM

On the hottest days of summer and the coldest days of winter I close the blinds. This helps to keep out extreme weather. But lately I've been closing them to keep out the eerie red light that's been overtaking the sky every evening. I get the feeling I'm living on Mars. I don't know if it's that volcano they're talking about or good old air pollution, the kind I grew up with and of course survived. I've noticed a lot of people out there with their cameras, and even a few painters trying to capture the unusual color. It won't last.

But spring is finally here, following a pretty treacherous winter, so I have been consumed by planning. I'm planning my battle tactics for my war against crabgrass, grubs, and black spot. Last year I got the tomato blight pretty much under control, so I'm not as worried about that. My angle this year is to take them one day at a time, to never let them get the upper hand. These things just wait for you to blink; then it's all over. You've lost. That's not gonna happen this year.

ANNE

I woke up remembering a dream the other day. I don't know where I was in the dream, but I do remember that everything, inside and outside, was covered in a fine red dust. The disturbing thing was that I could not clean the dust away. If I brushed it aside, it simply returned, same as before. There was nothing I could do to get rid of it. I have had disturbing dreams before. This is nothing new. But the worst part of the dream occurred not while I was sleeping, but later that morning.

The ground had finally thawed so I had planned to plant my onion sets. I made myself a good breakfast of steel-cut oats and cream, had a cup of tea, and bundled up to go outside. The air had a distinct chill in it, and it wasn't until I looked up, to the low hill where I would plant the onions, that I noticed it had snowed during the night. The snow, light and already melting, did not gleam at me like all other snows. It was a subdued snow, almost invisible. When I picked up a bit of it in my hand I noticed it was not very white. It was dulled, earth-toned. From where I stood, looking out over the fallow gardens, it almost seemed to have a reddish tint to it. Very strange. Was there that much pollution in the air?

I went ahead and planted the sets—thirty-two rows of them, and when I was finished I stood up, my back creaking, to survey my work. I always get a wonderful feeling after I plant my first vegetable of the season. The snow had melted and the air was warming. But very soon some light clouds blew in, almost as if they had been in hiding. As they shadowed me I looked up and saw their soft, translucent edges. And though it was mid-day they appeared to carry some of the previous night's sunset in them: a pretty, dusty pink.

TOM

I spent the better part of my day in the garden, a little disappointed by the chilly weather. Seems it should be warming up more by now. But once I got going I was on a roll—removing dead twigs and branches, defying emerging weeds, and raking out the brown grass. Then I got to spreading my Weed'n Feed when Olivia came by and asked what I was doing.

Her partner was away visiting her parents in Michigan, and Olivia seemed to have a lot of time on her hands. I didn't. She became very chatty with me. We discussed the benefits and drawbacks of perennials versus annuals, wild animal control, and the weather. I noticed her eyes moved often in the direction of my lawn and the spreader I was holding.

What's that?

Just my late-spring Weed'n Feed.

Oh. Is that…chemical?

I guess. If that's what works.

But you really don't want to do that, do you?

I certainly do. It works like a charm.

But the environment! That stuff gets into the water supply.

It's regulated isn't it? I mean, I put up my little yellow sign the way I'm supposed to every year.

Just because it's regulated doesn't mean it's okay. Why don't you come over to see our yard sometime? We use no pesticides or chemicals, and everything is healthy and growing.

I decided to put this to rest; I didn't want her coming around to lecture me every time she saw me doing yard work. So I accepted her invitation immediately, and we marched right down to her house.

Oh! Diane left that there.

Olivia lifted the wheelbarrow onto its wheel and pushed it into her open garage.

Don't you have a compost pile? I asked, seeing that the wheelbarrow was full of weeds and trimmings.

We do, Olivia replied, offering no more information about where it might be, or when she would take to the task. As she was arranging the wheelbarrow back into its hiding place I turned to survey the yard. The first thing I noted, but for the uneven grass, was a wall of hydrangeas suffocating the back of the house. They had obviously not been shaped in years, if ever. The house, yellow, was stained with streaks of greenish mildew.

It's the linseed oil, she said.

Excuse me?

The house stain has linseed oil in it, and the mildew feeds off it. I don't really mind though. Looks kind of rustic.

I guess so. You could try power washing it.

Power washing? Oh. Come see our vegetable garden.

She led me behind the garage, where a set of six small raised beds neatly contained many shades of young greens. At first I couldn't tell if they had been weeded properly, though I couldn't determine what kinds of weeds were intruding on the vegetables.

We like to plant things that get along together. Like the native Americans did.

Does that mean you dug a dead fish into the soil?

Not a dead fish, but we do use fish emulsion.

I can smell it.

The rest of the yard was, as far as I could see, a mess. Nothing tended to at all. We might as well have been in a meadow at the edge of the woods.

See our service berry back there? She pointed. That just came up by itself. I *love* when that happens.

Hmm. Maybe you should control that pokeweed.

Oh no, the birds love the berries. And we eat the leaves. You haven't heard of poke weed salad?

Yes, I've heard.

To each his own, I thought, and as the wind was picking up I decided to go. I thanked her for the somewhat interesting tour. She said we should discuss organic gardening sometime, looking up to the darkening sky. Just then I saw a few snow-flakes falling on my nose.

Oh! She said. Oh!

The snow continued, picking up speed, and we were both struck speechless for a moment: as the flakes spread through the air and gathered on the lawn, we couldn't help noticing that they were not white, but a distinct pink.

So late, she said, to be snowing. I wonder—could it be the air pollution?

ANNE

Everyone at the market was talking about the pink snow, even if it only lasted a few hours. And in the end it didn't seem to matter. All it did was make the ground wet, just like any other snow. And it's funny, the more I gazed at it, the less pink it became. I wondered if snow had been that color all along, and I only just then noticed it.

But others seemed to be struck more seriously by it. I don't often pay attention to the news, but it seems the current theory is that it had something to do with that volcano. As far as I know, it is still erupting. Small world, I guess. I still had some potatoes to sell at the market from last fall, but many of my regulars didn't show up. Hopefully they weren't panic-buying at Smart Shop, like everybody else! A little pink snow, and they've all gone nuts!

TOM

The last thing in the world I want, ever, is to be bothered by people who don't know what they're talking about. And they are everywhere. It's almost as if they offer degrees in bullshit somewhere. Or maybe there's some of that in all degrees? The annoying thing is not that people may think they know something; it's that they feel the need to share it when it's unsolicited. If I hear one more person telling me that the storm we had is going to drive food prices through the roof, well, I might just put my fist in their mouth. I mean, even if food prices do go up, I'll get along just fine by changing my eating habits and buying stuff that didn't go up. There are a lot of choices at the supermarket, and many of them are not perishable. Compared to what people had to do to survive centuries ago, it's no big deal.

Now my poor yard, that's another matter. The hail that came down piled up to a foot deep. It tore through any perennial that was up and on its way to summer, decimated every shrub, and virtually shut down the vegetables. I'll have to replant everything, even though we're well into May. Better than giving up, I suppose.

I remember a story my grandfather told me about a storm where he grew up, in Bavaria, nearly a hundred years ago. Snow fell for days, so deep it covered trees at the top of the mountains. Others, in the lower regions, snapped and fell onto one another like dominos, scaring the animals out of the woods and onto the people's farms. My grandfather awoke to find a family of wild boar in his kitchen: they had come in through a door the wind had blown open. So what did he do? He ate them, of course! They would not have stood much of a chance back in the wild, as it took weeks before the woods came back to life.

Any time I think we've had bad weather, I think about his story. He made the best of his situation. You might even say he spared those boar from starving to death.

ANNE

Walt came over that night and we drank a bottle of wine together. Actually two. I was crying, because I knew my little farm would never be the same. I felt as if my whole history were being wiped away when I saw that foot of ice fall. It encased everything, dead and alive and just awakening, and silenced it all in one fell swoop.

It won't touch us, he said.

Of course it touches us. It touches my soul. I grew up with the earth. If it's distressed, I'm distressed.

Listen. I've been collecting stuff for a quarter of a century. There's nothing I can't deal with if I use human ingenuity. Without it, let's face it, we wouldn't be here, hail storm or not.

I couldn't help it, I fell in love with Walt. I loved his scraggly beard and the dirt under his fingernails. I loved the focus in his blue eyes, and the work in his hands. Most of all through, I think I loved that I still knew next to nothing about him, and that I didn't need to know anything more than what I saw. He came gift-wrapped. And he lived right down the road.

Another thing about Walt: he never asked me much about my past, either. Not that I wouldn't have been happy to tell him about it, but it just didn't seem to matter to him. That's nice. What does it matter anyway? We are all growing continuously, pruning our experiences and cultivating new ones. I change with the landscape.

Let me know if you need a hand removing some of that broken brush out there, he said. At least we can pile it up and burn it.

TOM

I don't own a dog, nor a cat, nor anything else that might keep me up at night or make my nose run. I wear a mask when I do yard work, and keep the house spotlessly clean. So why, all of a sudden, do I have allergies? The doctor gave me some pills to take, and they work, but I feel like crap. I'd rather get to the bottom of it, and get rid of them once and for all. They gave me a list of things I'm supposed to be allergic to, like tree pollen and cat dander, but I HAVE NO CATS. And trees don't bloom all year. I have the same symptoms in the dead of winter. What's that about?

Another thing I seem to be battling lately is my rumbling GI tract—the whole thing, from start to finish. Seems there is hardly anything I can eat that doesn't leave me either with cramps, bloating, or flatulence. Usually, it's all three. I'm not guessing it's a sign of getting on in years either. There has to be something else to it. I'm guessing it's the way they grow our food these days, or the newfangled things they put in it. I know this because I'm not the only one who has these problems. They're practically epidemic.

On the other hand, we've wiped out a lot of diseases that killed our ancestors, and we're on the way to beating cancer. Should I be happy?

ANNE

I know I'm starting to run down a little. I chalk it up to getting a bit older. Like anything, it's a journey. But seems like no matter what anyone says you're not prepared for it. I imagine it's the same with having a baby. I decided long ago that I'd embrace aging. That's a hard thing to do, but I can't think of another way to stay sane while watching my face shrivel up, arms grow spots, and knees decide when they will and won't work. I know it's all illusion anyway, and the most important thing—my mind—is full of experience and better equipped to cope and make decisions than ever before. It's what they call peace of mind, I believe, and that's worth any number of wrinkles and brown spots.

Walt, though, didn't believe me. He said I looked a little more run-down than I should. He said it in a nice way. So I went to the doctor, something I rarely do. They sent me to the blood lab and took vial after vial out of me. A week later I got a call. They said I had Lyme disease.

The first thing I did of course was to read everything I could about it. I found so many sources on the web that I nearly lost my mind trying to decipher and distill all the information. I even read that the tests they give to determine if you have the disease aren't always accurate. I began to feel that I might have Lyme disease and I might not. That I could deal with it either way. After all, when you're sick you just have to adjust your attitude a bit, come up with a new daily routine. Then you begin to feel normal again. A lot of it's in your head.

In my case, I rethought every part of my day: what time I woke up and got out of bed, what I had for breakfast, how many breaks I took in my garden work, what I chose to read and how often, whom to see, whom to avoid. Every detail of my days affected my health, and I was careful not to compromise it. Walt, who never seemed to age or show any sign of his health failing, often asked me about these subtle changes in my daily routine. Oh, you're not eating bananas now? I don't remember that you ever took a nap before.

Feeling pretty good after making these adjustments then, I was well equipped to deal with some bad news I read on my laptop one morning. Crops were crashing all across the country.

I'd noticed that my tomatoes, cucumbers, and pole beans were stressed—in an odd way I couldn't put my finger on. Funny that everything should be affected at once. The usual suspects (bugs, fungus) were not present. The only thing that had changed much was the sunlight. By that I mean that there didn't seem to be much of it. I had missed the clear dawns of spring; they had been eclipsed by a grayness that sometimes lingered until mid-morning, carrying a chill with it. What to do?

I weeded. I weeded all day, carefully tilling around my damaged plants. The weeds, as usual, didn't seem to be as bothered by this gray spring. Although some of them, like the crabgrass, did have trouble germinating, the chickweed and purslane were happily chugging along. But even the trees leafed out unevenly, and quite a few just gave up and died. That was disturbing.

Thankfully I could still bring my lettuces to the market, and my customers were happy to find me among the empty stalls. Peas were thin and scarce; the asparagus barely inching upward. It seemed the bees were hiding and the flowers un-willing to show themselves for fear of being able to collect enough of the sun's rays.

The news reports worsened. Crops were crashing all over the northern hemisphere, and food prices were rising rapidly. I checked what I had in store: a few potatoes from last fall, a squash or two, and the vegetables I had put up in the freezer. I also had pasta, jarred fruit preserves I had made, and two shelves full of my tomato puree. I never liked eating processed foods, so I had next to nothing of those, mostly a few cans of organic soups. Of course I could buy food at the steep prices, or change my eating habits, but for how long?

TOM

Now they say tuna are being over-fished. As if that's all we have to worry about. I've also read that they are cloning to produce lab-raised foods—even tuna! Now there's an interesting solu-tion. I was never a big tuna eater, canned or fresh. But I've gotten used to it. I've noticed others have been eating more of it too, so I do my shopping very early in the day. They stock shelves at night.

Olivia and Diane have two cats. I've seen Olivia, the tall one, walking them on leashes. Nuts. Yesterday she stopped to chat with me (as she often does) as the cats sniffed at my feet.

I've been giving them table scraps. Mostly protein, she said.

As in meat?

And fish, especially tuna. They seem to be doing fine.

Saves you money.

That too.

Why don't you just get rid of them?

Oh no! We couldn't do that. They're *family.*

They're cats.

Listen, we're trying to organize a community food bank.

For the poor?

No, not really. For everyone. Things may get worse, and we want to develop a strategy for coping with it.

We have StopWatch.

That's fine, but we're all in this together. The whole world, not just the U.S., or this part of the country. We need to work together.

I'll think about it.

Come to the meeting this Sunday. Seven o'clock at the town hall.

I thought I had the wrong night. Was it bingo night maybe, or were they laying off teachers again? All the seats were taken. Olivia stood at the mike. She looked pretty calm, as if she could have been addressing a whole continent and it wouldn't have made any difference. Her demeanor in no way reflected her message though: our Earth was roller-coasting its way to hell, and we had no choice but to go along for the ride. What would we do about it? It was no use planning alone; it won't work. Any attempt at barricading yourself away from the rest of humanity could only result in ruin.

Whoa.

I raised my hand: We can't just sit around and wait. It's human nature to want to protect yourself.

She responded: Mother nature is bigger than we can imagine. And we aren't always her top priority.

So?

You think you can take her on?

No. But I can try, just as people have done for hundreds of thousands of years.

And most of them perished. We don't have to. We can get organized and adapt.

I noticed Diane was up there too, peeking out from behind the curtain. Another woman chimed in:

I don't care about anything but having enough affordable food to eat. And I mean real food, not junk.

Everyone looked up, not surprisingly, since everyone knew about eating. That at least was non-negotiable and not subject to shifting priorities. Olivia went on with her food bank idea, then added something about posting leftovers on a web site, a place where the neighborhood could find free prepared food. I raised my hand again:

And what would the criteria be for handing out this food? How would you prevent someone from hogging it all?

I guess that would be up to the person handing it out, according to need!

I fell mute. She knew I didn't buy it.

Because really, what choice do we have? If there is greed among us, it won't survive. It will be weeded out eventually. Those who are most willing to share will set the new standard.

It was beginning to sound religious. And I didn't necessarily think that was a bad thing, but I already had a religion, and I wasn't in the market for another one.

So I left, I pretending to take a phone call, but instead ducking out as fast as I could without looking conspicuous. Because I had walked to the meeting, I had plenty of time to think during my way back home. It was another chilly evening, the year of an absent spring. Even the air seemed confused, ready to burst into summer but hanging on to the weight of winter dampness.

I opened my door and was met by the same chill. So I opened a bottle of scotch and poured a little into a glass to warm me. It wasn't quite enough though, so I ended up making a fire. It took a while to get going but then I sat in my reading chair with my scotch and watched its flames rise and fall. And as I sat there, taken by the fire, I wondered how long it had been since I'd been to Mass.

For so long I had been trying to see it as an adult, to change my way of thinking about going to church. Shouldn't it make more sense now? Every minute of it defensible? But I finally threw in the towel: I am not a theologian, nor a seminarian. I'm simply one of the flock of graying sheep, keeping an eye out for anything that dislodges me.

When I was a child I took it all in. I didn't know I was trapped every Sunday morning or First Friday of the school year. Mass was predictable, but the drawn-out parts, such as the consecration and homily, never got easier. They were a discipline, like brushing your teeth. One hour seemed like five.

Now my life is full of other disciplines, and they are no less irritating. But I will not let them go, or I will be that lost sheep, no one in the distance, and miles upon miles of green grass that would give new meaning to aimlessness and boredom.

Did I want that?

ANNE

I couldn't help it. I took half of my jarred tomatoes to sell at the market, and I only charged half price for them. I count it as one of the best things I've ever done. They sold out in a half-hour, all thirty-five of them.

When I got home Walt was there, reinforcing one of the leaky walls in my shed. He didn't see me at first as I stood by the door, and I watched him for a couple of long minutes, his strong, determined body under a head of gray hair. Just the sight of him put me at ease, as if nothing bad could happen to me as long as he was there.

Storm coming up, he said. I shrugged.

No, it's a big one.

So I've heard. Maybe a warm front coming through?

Hardly. They're saying snow.

Snow! Well, there go the tomatoes and beans.

And okra and peppers, he added.

Forgot about them. Let's cover them up.

The storm will last for days, cold every night. They don't stand a chance.

We can't watch them die, Walt.

He looked at me the way he sometimes does, with those wise, mournful eyes. The truth is, neither of us knew what to do. Who is ready for snowstorms in June? So I dragged out what burlap covers I had and covered at least some of the crops. There was no harm in trying.

We awoke to the smell of fire, though through the dim light of a snowy dawn we saw none. The snow came down lightly, covering in powdery blankets the pack of two or three feet that drifted randomly as far as we could see.

The fire smell was from all the fireplaces that had been going since electricity had failed some hours earlier. Walt and I only lit up our pot belly when we rose. The shed had the feeling of being tucked inside the cove of a roaring ocean, with a dampness that cut through everything living and still. A mist pervaded the shed as well, making no distinction between interior and exterior air.

With the stove lit and the darkness barely lifting we went back to bed. Walt quickly drifted off again, while I could not let go of my senses. The roaring cracks of falling trees, unable to withstand a snow that weighed down every one of their fresh green leaves; the elusive whistling of the wind; the smell of smoke everywhere; and the chill that numbed my nose added to an excitement I had never before experienced.

I had always felt intimate with nature, but I was surprised that even when she was most threatening I felt at ease. Could it have been that I felt that way only because Walt was there? I think that, if I had been glued to a television set full of frenetic, repetitive voices I might have been a nervous wreck. But, being where we were, with nothing but our wits to protect us, I felt blessedly safe.

TOM

I spent most of the evening and night bunkered down in my basement. The lights flickered once or twice, then went out. So I could no longer track the storm on the TV news. Luckily I had a battery-powered radio, but reception was pretty bad. So I lay down there on my futon and listened to trees falling outside. One, I'm sure, nearly missed my house. But when I peeked out the window all I saw was black.

The next morning I awoke to a stillness that made me wonder if I'd gone to the next world. And when I opened the front door I was sure I had: soft waves of undulating snow drifts spread untouched over the neighborhood, broken only by fallen trees. The sky was smoky gray, and the last flakes danced in the air.

Then the sirens began. They came from all directions, though many of the streets must have been impassable. I wondered if they had plowed the main avenues that bordered my neighborhood so they could pass. My next thought was to build a fire in the living room's hearth. I had brought in three large piles of wood before the storm hit, but wondered how long it would last.

With the fire going I grabbed a protein bar to chew on while planning my day. I had food and water, and my gas stove would work if I used a match to light it. The biggest task would be shoveling the heavy snow while keeping an eye out for falling tree limbs, which I could hear coming down at regular intervals.

ANNE

Walt went to get more clothes, and blankets, for us. I watched him walk out to his truck, like a dark smudge in the air. The truck sputtered and lifted gently off its soft mound of snow, then made wide, deep tracks that were black in the gray air. With Walt gone I noticed the silence that had overcome the landscape. My gardens could not speak, could not clue me in to their progress, a progress cut short in one night.

Strange, I fell to inaction. There was nothing I wanted to do that had not already been done. I saw no point in trying to go anywhere. Others, I was sure, had fallen to that task. Occasionally I heard sirens in the distance, but none ever came close. The snow was already melting, but the devastation remained. So rather than pit myself against this all-consuming act of nature, I simply sat in my shed and read. I chose a book I hadn't read in a long time, but cherished as one of my favorites: *The Little Prince,* by Antoine de Saint-Exupéry. I felt a particular kinship with the Prince—he on his strange little planet, me on mine. I lost myself in that book as the fired died out and the day grew warmer.

It wasn't until early afternoon that I noticed Walt had not yet returned.

Walt was never one to lose himself in electronics. He ruled his universe and wouldn't let anyone or anything wrest that control from him. So I wasn't surprised that he didn't answer his cell phone. He often got sidetracked too, even at the most inopportune times, so there was no telling where he might be.

With the weather warming a bit I decided to set out walking. Normally I could reach Walt's house in twenty minutes. But that day, with the snow and slush and fallen tree limbs blocking the roads, I didn't know how long it might take. So I grabbed a granola bar and bottle of water and set off.

I'd often wondered how it would be if I could experience all the seasons at once, and that day it seemed my wish had come true. I was both enthralled and unnerved by it. The sky contained all shades of gray, blue, and white. In one direction white streaks stretched randomly on the horizon; in another a ball of gray hung and would not budge.

I stepped over twigs and branches of all sizes, with only a couple of pick-up trucks hedging their way along the road. The snow was melting into oddly compacted shapes, as if they were inhabited by creatures encased in white molds. Many times I had to step around them, and each turn brought a new perspective in a universe that had lost its sense of color. Budding green leaves lay fallen in the snow. Violets bled from the sky and softened into an orange mist. Trees limned in green lichen had split open to show their pale pulp. It was heart-breaking.

Most of the time I walked with my head down in order to navigate the chaotic debris. Then I looked up to see Walt's white house smudged in the distance—occluded, I'd thought, by the mist. But soon I discovered that the mist was snow, a new round falling heavily and making its way toward me. I felt I was walking through a gluey quicksand, and that I would never reach my phantom destination. Soon the snow reached me, pelting my face from all directions.

When I finally reached his house, the light was blinding. I couldn't tell up from down. I stood in his beautiful junkyard and took it all in—the continuous outline of everything: heaps of metal objects, crooked piles of wood, antique trucks and cars, and ancient fruit trees—all shadows of white. Then I approached the front door, knocked twice, and entered.

A fire burned slowly in the hearth, his cat Goliath sat snugly before it, and there lay Walter on the floor, stone dead.

TOM

I started shoveling early, around 7 AM, when the snow had let up and the wind had calmed. I looked up and down my street, where many tall oaks grew, and saw most of them dismembered beyond recognition. The planet had changed while I slept. This new world was something I'd never seen: a frightful confusion of snow, fallen branches full of green and white leaves, random lines of dangling utility wires, and immobilized cars. The only way to attack it was one shovelful at a time, so I got to work without further delay.

But the snow, though it appeared to be light, was heavy. It stuck to my shovel, my boots, and my clothes. I had only cut a narrow path from my door to the road when I noticed a purple hat bobbing up to meet me. Under it was Olivia's face. She was holding her iPad.

Hey there.

Hi Olivia. Some snow, huh?

That's why I'm here.

What?

Remember? You signed up for the relief plan.

Oh. Yeah. But first I need to shovel out my car.

Don't bother. None of the roads are passable.

How can we help anyone if the roads aren't open?

Plenty of ways…

She began rattling off her list of tasks and volunteers who had already claimed them, but I was only half-listening, because I just wanted to get back to my shoveling. I did notice though, out there in the crisp sunlight, that she had lovely skin. I admit I lost track then of what she was saying; something about her words did not match the lovely lips that were producing them. But neither of us could continue the conversation, because out of the blue we heard a distressed man's call for help.

It came from my neighbor Evan. Help! he cried. My wife's in labor!

Olivia and I looked at each other. For once she was speechless. There was nothing in her notes to accommodate this. So instinctively we trudged over to Evan's house, two doors away. None of his driveway had yet been shoveled.

Evan held the door open, and Olivia rushed in to locate his wife, Elena, who was pacing the living room with one hand on her back and the other over her sequestered baby.

Call the doctor! Olivia shouted.

I did that, Evan shot back. He's making his way to the hospital. But how are we going to get out of here?

By now a few others from the neighborhood had congregated on the road, which was being plowed by a neighbor enough for vehicles to pass in one lane. I turned around and began shoveling frantically. The others followed, and within ten minutes we had cleared a path to the road. Olivia peeked outside and shook her head:

She won't be able to walk up to the main road. Will the ambulance make it down?

What ambulance? I asked.

I called 911.

At that moment we heard a siren in the distance. All heads turned to look up our street. Red flashes painted the snow. In the next moment Elena screamed: Get me outta here! I looked at Evan.

Do you have a sled?

A sled? Yes, but it's in the garage. We can't get to it. I mean it would take all day.

I looked to my right and saw the cargo box that sat on top of his Subaru.

We'll use that.

Before Evan could say anything the others surrounded the car and began unfastening the cargo box. I went into Evan's house to find some large pillows. I saw only a few small ones, so I took the cushions right off the couch and threw them outside, followed by the pillows.

The cargo box was already on the ground, and we began arranging the cushions and pillows inside it. Evan appeared with a long rope, which he tied to the front of the box. Olivia helped Elena down the snowy steps as the community cleared the path to the road.

Our entourage was able to transport Elena to the waiting ambulance within a few minutes. We watched as they loaded her onto their more professional gurney, inserted her (and Evan) into the vehicle, and lumbered away. On the way back down our street to return Evan's cargo rack we were met by his elderly next-door neighbor, who presented us with a bottle of whiskey.

ANNE

The wind was kicking up again outside, along with the light snow, bringing waves of light into the room. I covered Walt with a blanket and sat there in the living room with him, listening to the quiet and occasional whistling gusts. Goliath looked at me, then turned his attention back to the warm embers of the hearth. We sat there for hours, until the light dimmed from the sky and the snowy glow was all that was left to brighten the world. Then Goliath and I curled up on the couch together, and fell asleep.

I was awakened by the chatter of dozens of blackbirds that had descended on the yard. I looked out and saw them pecking through the melting snow, as confused as the rest of us about this strange weather.

I wondered about Walt. He had no family that I knew of, and he was unconventional in everything he did. Should I leave him there where he died? Contact the state to dispose of him? Offer him up the gods? It struck me that his fate was in no one's hands but mine. I felt we were the only two left in the world. What was the proper thing to do?

Above all, I wanted to express our love, to honor it, uncommon as it was. I wondered what would become of his house, and of all the objects he lovingly collected—junk to everyone but him. Now that he was gone, what use did it have?

I decided I must take one thing, and turn the rest to ashes. Goliath, I decided, could fend for himself. He made for the trap door Walt had fashioned, on his way to his cat haunts, as if to tell me I wasn't needed. I meandered through the chilly house—some rooms only had plastic sheets for windows—and ended up in what most resembled the kitchen. Walt made his food there, but he made other things there as well, things of wood and things of metal, things made of all the things we throw away. One of my favorites was a bubble-wrap chair (too big to carry back with me though) but I also liked the things he carved from wood. I think he spent much of his day carving, and sometimes he would sell his carved salad servers and planters and canes by the side of the road.

The kitchen had a long table which I believe he made also. It doubled as a dining table and workbench. And since only a small surface was needed for his meals, the table was mostly stacked with all manner and shape of wood: walnut, maple, birch, cherry, and ash were some that I recognized. The table itself he made of wormhole chestnut from floorboards in the attic.

I sat at the table, feeling that I had become one of his carved objects, filled with his love. Then it occurred to me that I was nothing if not a miracle, my essence fueled by what he had given me, and was giving me still. His hands had formed me, but unlike the other objects he had formed I could take his love further, remove it from danger, plant its seed wherever I might go.

So I needed to take nothing from that house. I went back to the living room to where red embers smoldered in the fireplace. And using the little metal shovel I took those embers and spread them about the rooms. Within a few minutes small flames developed, and I left.

Looking back from the road once or twice I saw that the flames licked the windows, and would soon overcome the whole house.

TOM

They had plowed our street by mid-afternoon the next day, enough for two-lane travel, and I decided to take my little pickup out for a ride, if only to survey the damage. The sky had broken, reflecting its blue light everywhere in the snow. I was surprised to see a lot of people out walking, some even skiing or snow-shoeing. The roads were rough but passable.

I turned up the main avenue toward the grocery store, and saw that quite a few others had the same idea. But since the store's lots were not completely plowed there wasn't much chance of parking. So I went on, happy enough to see the beauty in this disaster as I looked around.

I decided to get away from the strip mall, and turned up a long hill that led to an old farm I sometimes visited during the summer for vegetables. The snow was not quite as high there, though the road was rougher. I was proud of my faithful old truck for taking it on.

Up there on the ridge that offered a nice view of the city in the distance there was not a soul to be seen. The snow sparkled on every fallen twig, every leaning branch, some showing hints of emerald leaves. But the sky was growing darker again. The scene was beautiful, but strange. I was not completely comfortable with it, and might have been pondering it too much, because I nearly ran over a woman wearing a white blanket around her shoulders. She turned to look at me, and I was struck by the angelic look on her face. I couldn't tell how old she might have been. But then I had to try to pull over, because a fire engine was coming up behind me. It turned a corner before it reached me, and when I turned my head for a second in the direction it was heading I noticed a wide plume of grayish smoke rising behind a grove of pine trees. I slowed and pulled over a bit to watch it when the woman wearing the white blanket passed me by. I put down the window on the passenger's side and called out: Need a ride?

She turned to look at me, at first blankly, then smiling. Okay, she said, then hopped in.

Not exactly the best day for a walk.

Actually it's pretty interesting out here, don't you think? Almost apocalyptic. It bears witnessing.

I guess so.

And where are you off to?

Was going to the store but my plans fell apart when I saw what a mess parking was there, so I decided to take a little ride. Where can I take you?

I'm just up there, to the right.

Where? I don't see it.

No, it's set back from the road.

Oh. Just let me know when.

The road was getting pretty rough. It had barely been plowed. The wind was picking up too. I was beginning to wonder if I should be out in that mess.

What did you need at the store?

Just some basic…Lord, now my truck began making strange sounds, something like a screeching eagle. I gunned her a bit, but that only made it worse. So I pulled over.

Sorry, I don't know what that's about. Looks like we might both be walking.

Not far though. We're here. You're welcome to come in for a cup of coffee or tea.

Oh, that's not necessary.

No, but I can't just leave you out here in this mess, can I? My name's Anne.

Oh, nice to meet you. I've had kind of a rough day. Tom.

That was the strangest invitation I'd ever gotten. But I had no choice. I had to accept it. We headed through the snow in the direction of her house, which was the sorriest thing I'd ever seen, really just a shack with an awning sticking out of it. As we approached I asked her about the shell of another house that stood nearby. She said she had grown up there, that a meteor or something had struck it and set it on fire. I didn't ask for any more details. Seemed a little peculiar to me, but I guess stuff happens.

ANNE

I had been walking on air, the snow so light underfoot and my head as clear as a summer day, when a small truck pulled up beside me and a man asked if I wanted a ride. At first I didn't know what to say. It seemed I had been the only one alive for quite some time and the sound of another human voice threw me off course. But he looked pleasant enough, and I didn't want to seem unsociable, so I said yes.

We hadn't gone too far when, wouldn't you know it, his truck broke down. But we were close enough to my place, so I invited him in for a cup of tea.

His name was Tom, and it seemed a little strange to have any other man in my home but Walt. I was even struck by how different they were. Silly, I know, to think that all men were like Walt.

Now we weren't sitting there long drinking our tea by my pot-belly stove before we heard a loud creaking sound. It seemed at first to come from all over, but then we saw that one wall—the end wall near by bed—was buckling in. I was afraid the shed would come apart. But this Tom wasted no time in rushing over to inspect it.

We went outside and saw that a snowdrift was pressing against it. Tom tried shoveling some of the snow away, but the wall wasn't going to change its mind. So I told him about some two-by-fours that were lying on the ground around the back of the shed underneath an awning; he brought them inside and began shoring up the wall. I didn't know if it would last, but it kept the wall from coming down.

I thanked him, and he left. He'd said he'd seen me at the farmer's market; took him a while to figure that out. Said he'd bought some of my vegetables and they were good. His old truck seemed to be fine now as he drove away. That seemed like a nice ending for a hard day. But shortly after he left the wall came down, and I was left looking at the snow-covered and partly green landscape from inside my shed. It was as if I were looking out onto a dream. I stood there in awe for a few minutes before packing up my stuff. I had to move back into the inhabitable part of our old, burned-out house.

TOM

I admit I stopped at the farmer's market a couple of weeks later, knowing there would be slim pickings, to see how she was doing. I couldn't stop thinking about her living in that shack. Was she maybe a bit mad? Did she have any family? How did she get along?

But she wasn't there. Her stall was empty.

I thought of asking the others if she'd been there, but decided that might sound creepy. And after all, who was I to intrude on this woman's life? We'd only had a cup of tea together. I didn't even know her last name. Still, the day was sunny and warm, so I found myself driving in the direction of her place. I thought I'd just drive by to make sure it was still standing. I don't know why, but I felt responsible about it.

As I approached I saw that the shack had collapsed. My heart skipped and landed in my throat. I parked the truck and made my way down to it. Might she be trapped inside? Before I got there though I stopped; a flashing red light washed over me. It was coming from a police car, which was pulling quietly out of the driveway leading to the burned-out house.

ANNE

They asked me what I knew about him. What could I say? I said he was kind and honest, a little eccentric. Unassuming.

How long had I known him? Oh, I think less than a year. Was that possible? Were we lovers? Lovers? What do you mean? Are you asking me if I loved him? I suppose I did. I cared for him; I saw something unique in him. Pure. He seemed connected in a way. Connected to what? To creativity. To him nothing humans made was ever junk. He took all those things and re-fashioned them, adding a bit of nature's work in too. That was genius to me. Don't you see it?

Did I know he was dead? They found his remains inside his burned house. He didn't come back, I said. I knew something was wrong.

That was not a lie.

I am not a good judge. I can't judge others; I can't even judge myself. I live not day by day, but minute by minute. I did away with lies long ago. Anything I do passes first through my conscience, and anything I do is by necessity. I learned that mostly by experience, the way all things go in nature. If anyone believes I've done wrong, it means nothing to me unless I believe it myself. When you know right and wrong instinctively you give birth to empathy, and when you have empathy you don't mind living in this world, no matter how unwelcoming others try to make it.

After they left I sat and thought. I thought about how alone Walt was, about how he took pride in his work, how he took things that most people think of as meaningless and gave them a part of himself. I could find nothing more beautiful than that. And when he died, surrounded by the things he made, I could not see sending him off without them. I think they were his religion. So I became the priest at his last rites, turning him into flames.

TOM

I saw her sitting in a chair by the window in one of the rooms that was still standing, so quietly that I wondered for a moment if I should disturb her. She may have been ill, or preoccupied with something. That was none of my business. Just as I hesitated though she turned her head, as if knowing I stood outside the window, and smiled at me. Then she rose, and I met her at the front door.

The smell of fire never leaves a house, especially one that was never refurbished following the conflagration. Even the rooms that were still inhabitable seemed to have a shadow cast over them, as if always in the company of ghosts. The kitchen had collapsed with the meteorite, but she made me a cup of tea from a corner of the living room that she had set up as a serving station. The electricity somehow still worked.

I couldn't really tell if she wanted me to be there or not. Her face wore a peculiar expression, both peaceful and worried. She explained how her shack collapsed just after I'd left that day, and that she had not set foot in the house since the meteor incident. It was her house; it had been in the family for generations and she had many good memories of it. It broke her heart to see it half-ruined, but she had no choice but to live there. Did she have plans to restore it? No, there really wasn't any money, no insurance, nothing. I could look into it; I could help arrange… No, she was fine with it the way it was. She didn't need anything more. What was the point, she said. Why?

Why? Because it's not fit for human habitation.

She looked around:

But I live here. My history is here.

I scanned the room, and the charred doorway that led to the fallen parts of the house.

You can't see it, she said. My history. But it's here in this house, and it's my connection to the earth, just as much as the land is around it.

I didn't mean to intrude, I said. But the way things are going these days, do you think you can survive in a place like this? Alone?

Funny, I never feel alone. I have my friends from the market—buyers and sellers—and just knowing I have them is good enough for me. But it's more than that; it's everything I've learned as well.

At school?

I never went to school. At least not a school building. I was taught by my mother.

Home schooled?

Yes. And that was the most liberating education I could have had. My mind was free to wander, be curious and ask questions about everything.

And your mother had all the answers?

Of course not! But we would search for them together, and we wouldn't let up until we understood what we needed to know. I guess that feeling keeps me from feeling alone too. There is always something wonderful about this world to investigate. You can never know everything.

Be that as it may, you're going to need heat next winter.

I'm not afraid of the cold. I have plenty of firewood.

In the twenty-first century?

Still works, doesn't it? More than you can say about a lot of things.

It was nice to see you again. Mind if I drop by again sometime?

No, I don't mind. Guests are always welcome here. Or see me at the market?

Yes.

I don't know why. I came home, unpacked a few things I'd bought at the drug store, left them lying on the kitchen table, and sat down. I sat there for hours I think; not hungry, not angry, nor happy. Not anything really. Just sitting there.

Why hadn't I mentioned the police car to her? Why didn't she mention it to me? It was at the top of my mind when I met her at the door. Then it evaporated, as if it had never happened. She had that power over me.

The next day I took a long walk in the woods. I hadn't done that since I was a kid. The ground was squishy and it annoyed me. But I found a path that led to higher ground, and lots of rocks to climb over. I'd forgotten how many different kinds of plants were on this Earth. This walk was an extension of the evening before, a personal prayer of sorts. I wasn't feeling sorry for myself; I just wanted some time to think about things—like why my wife had left me, why I didn't go to church any more, why I needed to go to the woods for the first time in many, many years.

I was tired of my neighborhood, tired of human drama, tired of trying to make things work, just tired. And then along comes Anne, and I don't know which side is up any more. I no longer believe in my past, in the choices I've made. I've learned nothing, know nothing. It comes as a great surprise to me, and a great relief.

ANNE

I kept hearing voices, all night. I didn't know if they were night owls, raccoons, or some other creature, but they spoke as if in words. They became the voices of my mother and father, then the voices of my childhood friend Mary, and the voices of my friends at the vegetable stand. They made the night sweet, and I awoke with a smile on my face.

I sipped my tea, but my heart had sunk. Everyone I knew had become a phantom, unreachable, leaving me to wonder if I had ever really known them. How did I know I hadn't just dreamed those I'd loved? Why was it I couldn't take them for granted, as I did the plants in my garden?

I packed up my scallions, peas, and mesclun and headed to the market, feeling detached from everything I had once thought dear. For the first time in my life I felt I was on auto-pilot, so familiar with my task that I forgot why I was doing it. I stood by my wooden stand and saw not the pattern of the wood but the grimy marks where years of organics and violent weather had stained it. I wondered at the faces of my fellow vendors. What kind of lives did they have outside of this grim Saturday morning? What confessions would they make at the end of their lives; what secret ecstasies had they encountered simply by knowing others like them existed, and shared their uncertainties?

I wanted to throw my arms around the world at that point—not the world of mud and standing trees, but the world of colorful garments, of pop music and bumper stickers and ice cream. But I felt these things were beyond my reach, even if I knew where to find them. I had become too detached.

I went back to Walt's house. I saw that we were forever connected. Our houses had burned; things we had once thought valuable were gone. Those reflections of our lives up in smoke, not much remaining. But I was there to see the ashes. He was not. He had gone up with his house. I remained.

Then, an intruder. Someone disconnected, who didn't belong in my thoughts, let alone among the charred wood and collapsed furniture. He eyed me, held me long in his gaze. I felt I had nothing to say to him, nothing to share. But he approached. He said something, but I interrupted him. You don't belong here. Excuse me? You don't belong here. What are you doing? Looking for evidence. Forensics. Evidence of what? Foul play. Did you have any connection with the deceased?

I laughed. I laughed again. I laughed until I couldn't laugh any more. I don't know why. The idea of him standing there, so utterly uninvolved in Walt's life, asking me if I knew him. *Why?*

Do you live nearby, ma'am?

Yes, right down the road.

Are you Anne—?

Yes. I am.

I'd like to ask you a few questions.

I'm not in the mood to answer them.

I can wait a few minutes.

No, thanks.

Okay. In that case, when was the last time you saw your friend Walt Beacom?

Beacom? Was that his last name?

Yes.

Who are you?

Fire marshal Skrabski, ma'am.

You don't belong here. He's gone. His house is gone. There's nothing left. Nothing to talk about.

I'm here to investigate the cause of this fire and report to the county coroner.

I see.

Did you see the house as it was burning?

I live right down the road. And yes, I did see it. I was right here when it burned.

Were you? You watched it burn?

I'll tell you what happened. Walt was dead. He had no family that I know of, no friends, nobody. No one to send him off with dignity. So I did. I sent him off with dignity.

You mean you—

I did it with fire. I let it consume him, and everything he made.

That's a crime, ma'am. That's arson.

He owed nothing on this place. It had no value to anyone but him. What good could it have done standing here without him?

I don't make the laws. I just do my job. I'm sorry, but you can expect the police to come by with some questions for you.

I've already spoken with them.

And you told them what you just told me?

Not in the same words.

Thanks for your cooperation ma'am.

He walked down to his little car and left, just like that, leaving me to stand among the ashes.

As I was approaching my house I saw Tom's truck, but he was pulling away. I don't think he saw me coming. It was then that I began feeling that everyone was pulling away from me—Why? What had I done?

I stopped at my front door; I stopped and looked at that worn-out door. And a feeling of foreignness washed over me. I had never seen that door before like that: unfamiliar, stark, and uninviting. I felt like fleeing. But I had nowhere to go.

TOM

They're always throwing garbage on my front lawn: local rags of papers containing ads, the latest hullabaloo at the Rotary Club, a new list of rules for trash pickups. I just throw them into my recycling bin.

But today I threw our local chronicle onto the kitchen table along with an armful of junk mail. I put the gallon of milk I was holding in my other hand into the fridge. Then I turned around and looked back at the table. I saw Anne's face staring up at me from that paper. She had made the cover, because she had been arrested.

I skimmed the article, searching for an explanation. Arson? Maybe murder too? What house? She didn't set fire to her house; a meteor did. They had it all wrong. The wrong house, wrong Anne. Everything was wrong!

I sat at the kitchen table and stared at my coffee. The kitchen was unfamiliar. I had to fix what was unfamiliar about it, but first I had to find out what to fix. At one point I stood up, as if ready to fight. But there was no one there to fight, and I sat down, hoping no one had seen me. I finally understood what limbo was, that place between action and inaction. It was more frightening than either direction. Maybe I *could* save Anne.

But I had no conviction.

She opened the door before I knocked. I think she knew my footsteps. I brought dinner along with me—dinner for two, Japanese teriyaki steak with rice and vegetables. I didn't know if she ate meat, but she set the table for us, opened the boxes, and took some. She even produced a bottle of cheap wine, acting as if she had been saving it for a special occasion.

We ate quietly, so I had occasion to study her face, a paradox of earthly calm and heavenly aspiration. Many things could light up her mind, but it always returned to a kind of complacency—not bitterness, but acceptance. The mundane business of obtaining food, grooming her hair, and making a living was something that irked her, I believe, though she sadly and reluctantly surrendered to it.

So when she offered to pour me more wine, and I noted how nicely she had set the table with embroidered cloth napkins and fine china, I took it as an honor and a compliment. I hadn't thought she ever paid attention to such things. In fact, I nearly forgot the reason I had come. Was it to discuss the charges brought against her as I had seen them in the paper? Was it to comfort her in the face of adversity? Perhaps a little of both? Was I to give her advice, lend an ear, or pretend I knew nothing?

Strangely, I believe she heard all these questions as they rolled around in my head. And, just as I could not determine which was the most valid, or pressing, I think she would not have known how to answer any of them. So we sat, and ate, and drank, and avoided the phantom topic altogether. And as the hours wore on I became even more aware of the pain she bore. It was all I could see, and soon one thing became very clear to me: we would spend the night together.

Waking up in a house that is half burned down, looking out a window streaked by time and its generations to a garden plot lovingly tended but wrecked by an indifferent Earth, I felt I had shed something. It left me cold. So I put my arms around her as she slept, and I began to imagine her life.

She was pure in a way that I could never have been, unaffected by years of classroom toil, schoolyard pranks, and religious indoctrination. Yet she was as intelligent, wise, and spiritually aware as anyone I'd met. Like a messenger from a galactic civilization who had selected me as their only contact. Yet how could someone so alien to my experience on this Earth be so grounded and connected to it?

I think that's when I began to lose it: my religion. I don't mean losing everything I'd been taught, just losing the idea of keeping it in a bottle and shaking a bit of it out when you need it. That felt like hoarding to me. It also felt like anxiety, a constant fear of not knowing when to tap into it. I preferred something more constant, something I didn't have to catalog and reflect on, but that was an inherent part of me, a natural ethical sense. Was that possible to have? I doubt that I would have asked the question if I hadn't met her.

ANNE

There was something about his arms. They were sturdy in a way that I couldn't pinpoint. Not just strong in a masculine way, but also constant, reassuring. They were in contrast to the chaos of this world. They had grown sturdy with the man who owned them. I felt that the world could fail, but those arms wouldn't. They gave me permission to lose myself, and not feel lost.

When I finally awoke, with one foot in this world and one foot in my dreams, I saw him looking past me to the window.

Do you want some coffee? I don't usually drink it, but I'll make you some.

Only if you've grown it yourself.

Sorry. It's from the outdoor market though. Roasted by a friend of mine. Organic.

That'll do.

I scrambled some eggs for us too on my little propane stove. We ate quietly, a warm light spilling over us from the nearby window. I felt the limbo I had been living in recently dissipate, replaced by a realization that there was nothing wrong with the world.

So what about that article? he said.

I looked up, at once responsive and confused.

In The Chronicle.

The Chronicle?

You were arrested.

Oh. Yes, I was.

And?

My friends from the market took up a collection to bail me out.

Nice of them.

It wasn't a very pleasant experience.

I'm sure it wasn't. But—why?

A man's house burned down. He was in it. They think I killed him.

Did you know him?

I did. He had no other family or friends that I know of. So of course they are implicating me.

But why?

Because I burned the house down.

You—you burned it down?

He was in it. But he was already dead. I knew there would be no other way to dispose of his body. He wasn't religious. God knows what the state would have done with him.

But you might be found guilty, go to jail…

I did the right thing, Tom. Don't you agree?

It doesn't matter whether I agree. It's whether the state agrees.

Oh. I see. I guess I don't see it that way. What does matter to me though is what you think.

You need to reflect on this, Anne.

He was dead when I found him. I told you. Why should I be worried?

Because we live in a world where everything has to be proven.

Even the truth?

Especially the truth.

I'd make a bad lawyer.

Yes, you would.

ANNE

I was set to appear in court in July, when everything would be blooming in spite of the erratic spring we'd had. Until then I would be tending my gardens, tidying up what was left of the house, and watching the sun decline. Not much different from other springs, with one exception.

I was tired.

It wasn't that I was worried about the impending trial. I felt that I had come to a wall of sorts. A psychological thing? Maybe. Maybe, at the age of fifty, I had finally come to realize that my world view was not that common. My mother had always said it's not what you know, it's what you believe that counts. Trouble is, I never knew what I believed, only what I knew. Believing in something seemed artificial, dishonest. What you know, after you know it, is effortless; but what you believe, I guess, takes a lot of practice, something you build up from nothing, no definable source. I know very well how to grow onions, but I don't know how to reckon with a Creator who gives us no hints about why anything is created.

Tom came over more often, and I began to see something to believe in. It hovered around him, like a matrix of some truth that had been foreign to me. It made me forget my mortality, my connection to the earth. I felt I could rise above it, just by cultivating a conviction.

We took a walk in my vegetable garden. I was feeling very pleased with its progress, confident that I had planted everything in the best place to see it to fruition. But Tom saw it another way. He began asking me questions: why were scallions planted near tomatoes? Why cucumbers at the bottom of the slope? He said he didn't understand my logic.

My logic? I did have a logic. My logic was whatever works. It was mostly by trial and error, I explained, that I chose anything. Scallions are planted first, tomatoes much later. So I conserve space by planting tomatoes among the scallions, most of which I will eat long before the tomatoes ripen. Cucumbers don't like to dry out, so I put them where water doesn't evaporate as quickly. Each vegetable and flower has its own story. I am familiar with every one. Oh, he said.

But wouldn't I yield more crops if I planted them in numerous rows? Wouldn't it be easier to fertilize them and deal with pests that way? What if a row fails, I said, because the soil is a little different under part of it, or the pest is more prevalent in one part than another? What plants need is individual attention, not group therapy. My gardens are successful because I give them time, as much as they need. I'm out there every day. I nip problems in the bud. And I get high yields.

But you spend all that time.

Well, what else would I be doing?

TOM

Enough, I thought. I have always tried to see things from another's point of view. I am not judgmental. But Anne is delusional. She doesn't seem to realize how serious her situation is. But I didn't know what to do about it. So I found myself doing something I hadn't done in a long time. I went to church.

In my childhood church was a place to daydream. Even when I served as an altar boy, my mind was free to roam elsewhere. I saw it as a place where even adults had permission to step out-side of their lives and let everything go, as they all participated in re-enacting a mysterious, ancient play. At that time I wasn't capable of finding meaning in the play. I only knew that it was in some way comforting.

I went to a daybreak Mass, the kind I used to serve, when only a few people are in attendance, there is no music, and no real homily. I tried to return to my childhood and all the feelings I'd had then, when everything was in order around me, and Mass was a gift that allowed me freedom through that order.

But it didn't happen. I did find myself daydreaming, but I also found that this particular brand of daydreaming was no different than the kind I experienced in the shower, at the park, in a traffic jam, or in the middle of a dull book. What I needed was no longer escape. I needed to intrude, intrude deeply into my life, and Anne's, to find out what we had in common, what made us both cast from the human mold. I felt I had been running from myself my whole life, and I needed to put on the brakes. I was ready to accept whatever I might discover about myself, and others, that I had been neglecting. That kind of work leads to fuller living, while blind subservience leads to an infinite desert.

The Mass was over, I went in peace. But I stood outside the church for a few minutes, thinking. The young priest who said the Mass passed by, offering a terse hello. I headed for my car when the pastor, Father Meyer, whom I'd met while jogging occasionally, came walking across the lot. He stopped, smiled, and asked me how the running was going.

I haven't been running lately.

Injury?

No. I don't know why. I'm just taking a break.

I know what you mean. Sometimes you need to recharge your perspective.

That's an interesting comment coming from a priest.

I'm no different than you.

He smiled, but detected that I was a little preoccupied.

I was actually out for a walk just now. I too feel the need to slow down sometimes. Want to join me?

So I joined him. We walked down the little hill from the church to a suburban sidewalk, then made our way to a path that circled a reservoir lake.

I haven't seen you at early Mass before, he said.

No, I usually don't go then. Actually I don't go very often. Sorry about that.

Nonsense. That's better than most.

I'm—sort of—wondering about the whole thing. About the ritual, what it means. I was an altar boy, and the experience I had back then is not what I'm having now.

Of course it isn't. You're not a boy any more. You get to call the shots now.

But I'm really doubting the whole thing.

You might be surprised to learn that I do sometimes too.

Really? Then how do you go on with it?

It's not hard to keep up appearances. Same as any profession. I'm not doing it for myself though. My job is to help others in matters of faith. That doesn't absolve me from my own struggle.

Okay Father. Can I level with you? Do we really need these stories any more? I mean, these days, aren't we more sophisticated in the way we can communicate and figure things out?

Figure things out. You're talking about physical properties, I assume?

Physical, biological, mechanical—everything. We're not in the dark any more for most things. And the rest we're closing in on fast.

I'll grant you that we do have a deeper understanding of many things, but I'm sure you'll agree we haven't come close at all in the most important ones.

You mean, why we're here?

I mean that and a host of more subtle things: feelings we have for one another, the power of memory, the choices we make. And let's not fool ourselves into thinking there is no such thing as evil. It hasn't gone away, and in some cases it's getting stronger.

But how do we agree on what evil is?

We nurture one another. We call it out. We don't let it slip by. If we're not sure, we talk about it. Evil is silence in the face of injustice, my friend. It is allowing things to go on when we're not comfortable with them. It's forgetting our powers of perception, those subtleties that make us more human and divine.

You're losing me, Father.

Oh, that's right. Spend too much time reading theology and that happens. Let me bring it back to earth: Is there anything at all you would defend, fight for, maybe even give your life for?

I guess there is.

Why?

Because I feel that strongly about it.

Why do you feel strongly about it?

Because, I guess, it is something that defines me. I am nothing without it.

Give me an example.

My family. My parents. My childhood. I don't know how exactly one defends a memory, but—

Exactly. You want to defend a memory because it defines you. You are nothing without it; you wouldn't exist. So you would fight for your existence. Life is powerful stuff. Yet we find some who convince themselves that it is a trifle. They don't know why they are alive; they can't explain it. So they deny its importance.

Are you talking about abortion?

I could go there, but I won't. People have trouble getting outside of their precious opinions about that. Let's stick to your life, mine—two that already have a big history.

There is something else I feel strongly about.

A woman?

You guessed it. But she's not your average woman.

How's that?

She lives alone in strange circumstances.

Oh?

She lives in the burned-out house she grew up in. She has no religion. She was home-schooled, and she has been accused of murder.

Father Meyer had no response at first, then he spoke:

Can you tell me a little more about that?

A friend of hers lived down the street—also a loner of sorts I think—and one day she found him dead in his house. Knowing he had no family or financial means, she took it upon herself to make the decision of how to release his body from this world. So she set the house on fire.

His house?

Yes. His house, which was about as dilapidated as hers, and full of junk. Thing is, she really doesn't think she did anything wrong. But of course it doesn't look so good to the authorities. How could they know she didn't kill him?

Do you believe she's innocent?

She is definitely innocent. She feels things deeply, and is committed to doing the right thing. But that's all based on the unique circumstances of her upbringing. Her sense of right and wrong. In a way I think she is more moral than the rest of us. I think that's why I'm struggling with my own religious upbringing. It seems wrong that I don't have the confidence and clarity that she has. But I'm rambling on now—

Father Meyer was old school, Vatican Two. Willing to listen, willing to go out on a theological limb for his parishioners. The younger priests were nothing like this. They touted the line, and gave no indication that they had personally thought about anything. It was very disheartening to me, who needs to think everything through and come to my own conclusions, especially about the big questions. But, much as I enjoyed my conversation with Father Meyer, in the end I felt no different. Maybe I was expecting him to clear everything up for me, even just a little. He didn't. We are all floundering, it seems.

His advice about Anne: do nothing. Let justice take care of itself. Maybe he didn't quite get the message that I was in love with her.

TOM

I arrived at her house early the following day. People were driving to work on a regular Wednesday morning. She was surprised to see me. My suitcase lay on the back seat of my car. Why, she said. Because we are leaving. Now? Yes, now.

I didn't know where we were going. I just drove. I picked north, a route I had taken before. Was there someplace she'd like to see? A place she had never been to? It didn't matter, she said, because she had never really gone anywhere. Except once. She remembered having been to Canada as a child. Where in Canada, she could not remember.

So we drove to Canada.

We drove up Route 91, through Connecticut and Massachusetts, into Vermont. We opened the windows and let the cool breeze ruffle our hair. A sparkling river, spotted with trout fishermen, ran in a deep ravine alongside the highway. There was so much to talk about, but we didn't say anything. We drove on through the afternoon and into the evening. When we finally passed the Canadian border, we were hungry, and stopped at the first little French restaurant we found in a town nearby.

I had not been to Canada very often, and even then only to the English-speaking parts. The waitress, however, handed us the English menus, so my fears were allayed. Anne, on the other hand, looked suddenly uncomfortable.

What's wrong? I said.

I don't know.

Must be something.

I think I feel lost here. On a different planet.

You are.

You know, I don't think I've traveled much outside New England.

Not even for family vacations?

Yes—we had a couple of those. I think we went to the Adirondacks once, and once here.

Then you've traveled.

But that was different. I'm not sure why. When my mother was there, it was different. Everything I saw, I saw through her eyes. She brought home with us wherever we went. She translated and interpreted the scenery, the people, the history. She was the only teacher I ever had.

I Don't think that's so different from what I grew up with.

You went to school, didn't you? You had a bigger social life, and a whole lot of teachers to translate the world for you.

But all under the roof of a particular system. It's the way I learned that evened it all out for me. There wasn't much I could do to break the mold of classrooms, all-powerful instructors, and exams. In a way I've been sheltered too.

I noticed she was not really listening.

So we can go two different ways from here. Into the woods, or into the city. I'm okay with either. How about you?

She hesitated, then softly replied: city.

Every now and then I realized the gravity of our situation. I was traveling with a person indicted with a felony, specifically second-degree murder. I was an accomplice in helping her leave town. We made it across the border through the negligence of the crossing guard on a small country road. And yet Anne's composure put me at ease.

So we went to Montreal. We called ourselves Ben and Linda. She held my hand tightly wherever we went. The first day there we walked around the cobblestone streets, watched street performers acting as mimes and posing as iconic statues. By evening we were tired and hungry, so we slipped into a small restaurant by the river. We spent a good deal of time perusing the menu, which offered some classical French dishes alongside more contemporary ones. A waiter came by, addressing us in French. And, to my surprise, Anne answered him in French so fluently that he didn't bat an eye. She ordered for both of us.

I didn't know you could speak French.

My mother's family were French. She taught me how to speak it. The grammar too.

So you can read it?

Yes.

Do you know any other languages?

Spanish, German, and Latin.

All equally well?

Pretty well. Maybe not as well as French. But I could get by.

That's amazing.

Why?

I don't know. Your mother must have had a pretty good education herself.

She went to Harvard.

Oh. I see. And why did she choose home schooling for you?

Because she didn't want me to experience the same shortcomings she had in her education.

But she went to a world-famous university. You didn't.

I knew I shouldn't have said that. I expected her to become indignant. But she didn't.

One thing my mother taught me, above all else, is that it doesn't matter where or how you learn something, as long as you learn it well.

But you need to be challenged by other minds, great minds, to learn something well.

My mother had a great mind. And she introduced me to other great minds through books.

Did you ever consider that everything you know has been colored by your mother's point of view? Wouldn't that prevent you from cultivating your own?

I asked a lot of questions during my upbringing. We consulted books together. A lot of what I learned, we learned together. We debated what we read. How many people do you need to have an honest dialog?

It wasn't that I wanted to prove her wrong. I just wanted to understand her better. She was so confident, so trusting and unaffected. In a way I didn't want to change her; I was afraid my prying might bring on some kind of personal crisis. But she never showed any sign of irritation or lingering sense of a shattered world view. Is that why I loved her?

ANNE

The day we looked out over the city, from Mont-Royal, I felt as if I'd been floating above the world. The French I had learned while walking the woods with my mother had been transformed into a new perspective, a living world that had been in hiding until then. I thought I had broken free, but I also felt lost. I gained a new sense for the immensity of the Earth; I knew I would never be able to see all of it. I took Tom's hand while standing there, hoping he would keep me grounded in that particular time and place. I was grateful he had brought me there, but afraid of being left alone.

We descended the hill back into the city. Tom pointed out an amusement park, which rose like a set of decorated cakes along the river. Here was another world within the French-speaking one we had found ourselves in. We entered the park, bought ice cream and waffles to eat, and walked through the wildly colored amusements, the French-sounding voices, the darting children and young couples. Tom led me through this kaleidoscope, and instead of feeling as if I were a part of it, I began to feel more and more anonymous, like a small fish under a teaming, silent ocean. I was both thrilled and saddened, but trusted Tom to lead me through. As the light began to fade I said, Tom I think I want to go home.

At the border it seemed the guards were distracted. They checked all the cars quickly, including ours. Tom found out there was a heightened terrorist alert, and there were specific individuals on the run from Canada. We obviously didn't fit the bill, so were waved on like everybody else. Tom seemed a bit nervous, as we saw quite a few police cars on the American side for the next several miles. They seemed to be stopping vehicles randomly. Tom drove the speed limit. But they pulled us over anyway.

Turns out we were going 65 in a 50 mile per hour zone. The officer checked Tom's license and gave me a nod. He took the license back to his car and sat there a while, talking on his phone. Then he returned in a hurry, told us to be more careful, and let us go. He sped off in the opposite direction. A line of flashing police cars, coming out of nowhere, followed him.

I dozed off as we passed through Massachusetts and into Connecticut. I felt myself suspended in a state of half-consciousness and dreaming. One moment I sat relaxed in Tom's car, listening to the road hum; the next I lost my footing as I made my way through a dark cave, reaching out for walls that weren't there, catching glimpses of light through crevices in the distance that disappeared when I blinked. At one point I must have jumped in my seat, for Tom said, Are you all right? I opened my eyes to darkness, still frightened.

Oh—It's getting dark.

Yes. You've been sleeping for quite a while.

Where are we?

We're pulling up to your house.

He drove slowly over the rocky yard, the headlights pointed at the front of the house.

What's that? he said. On the door.

I opened the car door and stepped back into my beloved, familiar world. Tom had already made his way up the three steps to the porch. He stood before the sign that had been posted on my front door. When I reached the steps he turned and said: It's condemned.

I knew what that word meant, yes, but I could not respond. I was condemned; my life was condemned. Who had the right to do that? I had come to terms with my mother's death, and Walt's. I had survived some unforgiving weather, and the fracture of our house. But to leave it would mean losing myself completely. I felt the earth give out from under me. I hit the ground as if crashing into another world. I remember hearing nothing but my own voice, the one word I spoke: *Tom!*

ANNE

I remember hearing his voice, the comforting cadence of it against the hum of his truck. We were going to his house. I had not been there before. We'll figure this out, he said. Don't worry.

I wondered: figure this out. Was it a math problem? A chart with holes to fill in? For a moment I wanted to jump out of his truck and find my way back home. He was taking me to another world, his world, and I would always be a foreigner there.

What do you think they'll do with my house?

I don't know. Tear it down? There's not much of it left.

It's my house. I grew up there.

I'm sorry, I didn't mean it that way.

The first thing I noticed when we entered his house was the crucifix hanging in the hallway. That was my mother's, he said.

The colors inside were dull, but calming. Tom kept out a lot of clutter. His magazines were stacked neatly in their rack. His slippers and shoes sat in perfect line by the door. One book, a novel, lay on the coffee table. It almost looked like a department store exhibit. Then I noticed a few other things: the small hummingbird feeder attached to the window outside by a suction cup, the bread maker in the kitchen, a couple of antique book stands that must have been heirlooms. These things told a different story, and somehow put my mind at ease.

We sat in the living room on a light green couch, and he held my hand. You can live here, he said.

I had never lived anywhere but where I was raised. The idea struck me as frightening, impossible, even humorous. So I did not respond. We sat there until the light grew dimmer. Tom switched on the lamp: I have something to show you.

He presented a letter from the Chief State's Attorney's office he'd found in my mailbox. It said my case had been dropped due to lack of sufficient evidence. I was exonerated of all charges.

Walt could rest in peace.

What happened next I find difficult to describe, because I tell it not from my own point of view, but from that of others who knew me. If I told it from my point of view, it would be a different story.

They say I became despondent, that I would seldom speak or acknowledge others in the room. I lost interest in cooking, even eating. I remember Tom pushing food in front of me, and how tasteless it seemed. I rarely left the house. If I found myself in the yard, I noticed not the grass and flowers, but the glaring sun. The longer I stayed outside, the less comfortable I felt. It was as if the earth had one aim: to swallow me. I found solace inside Tom's house. But even there I did not trust the air that wrapped me.

TOM

Sleep wraps most people in a veil of calmness. The day can bring anything it likes: anger, sadness, elation. But at night those emotions lose their strength, and evaporate.

With Anne, it was the opposite. I watched her face as she slept, the vertical crease in her brow, the eyelids clenched tight and cheeks quivering. I didn't want to wake her, because I felt it would do her harm. When she awoke it was as if someone had hypnotized her. She responded when I spoke to her, but seldom offered anything more to the conversation. I could read nothing on her face.

I didn't know what to do, so I did nothing but care for her for the following several weeks. Slowly she became acclimated to the house, setting the table every evening for dinner, even cooking simple meals. Once she brought in a few twigs of the flowering hydrangea from the yard and set them in the middle of the table. I complimented her on the choice. She smiled, but looked at the floor. Anyone who visited left with the impression that all was right: the house was in order, food well prepared, and conversation not contentious. Anne usually went to bed early, and seemed neither grateful nor irritated by the company.

I hadn't been to church in a long time, but that Sunday morning nothing seemed relevant—not the predictable newspaper, nor the tamed yard, nor the familiarity of my house. I wanted something more. So I told Anne I was going to Mass, and asked if she would join me. She looked at me with a short burst of concentration, like a hesitant squirrel, and said yes.

The church I went to was nice-looking, but nothing special. It had a vaulted ceiling with decorative wooden beams, simple windows containing insets of stained glass, refurbished recessed lighting over the altar, a new paint job, and a stone baptismal font.

I've never been in a church before, she said.

There are prettier ones.

She sat diligently through the Mass, reading along in the missal when she could, pondering a phrase or two before going on. I wasn't sure I hadn't made a mistake in bringing her. The priest's homily made no impression on her, but once or twice a smile crossed her lips during the recitation of some of the prayers.

Afterwards we walked to the car. I liked it, she said. I'd like to go again, maybe when it's not so crowded.

Sure, we can go again. I'm not a very good Catholic though. I don't even know if they still have Masses every day during the week.

Why week days?

You said not too crowded. Those early morning Masses on weekdays are generally sparse.

Oh. I'll go on Tuesday.

One thing though, Anne. You really shouldn't be taking communion.

Why not?

Because you're not a Catholic. It's a rule.

A rule?

Yes. There are lots of rules.

I see.

The weather was nice; fall was approaching. I embarked on my annual flower and vegetable bed cleaning: cutting down perennials, pulling up clumps of crabgrass, discarding spent bean stalks and other vegetables to make room for fall crops of spinach and lettuce. Anne was surprised to see my diligence in gardening. I had never really talked about it with her, partly because I knew she was a master gardener, and I was a mere hobbyist. But she jumped right in to help me, offering advice without condescension, and doing more than her share. I think the physical activity aided in her recovery, though I think the Catholic Masses, mysteriously, had something to do with it too.

ANNE

I was pulling weeds all morning, just as I had done thousands of times in my life, when I became annoyed. I did enjoy being outdoors, and feeling the sun on my back, but in an instant it seemed that what I was doing was futile. Indefensible. It was a never-ending battle, one that I could never win.

So I stood up and admired the flower bed I was trying to correct. But I couldn't see it. I saw only the flowers that had been spent, the grayish leaves wilting at the bottoms of their stalks, and the leaves mottled by fungus and voracious insects. I knew I should be able to take it all in without bias, but I couldn't. It was at that moment that I decided if I could not better the natural world, I would better myself.

Somehow I had believed that I was no better than a leaf or insect. I had my imperfections, yes, but that was something that came with the living—anything that lived. Insects and leaves, though, will go about their business bearing their bruises and imperfections, and think nothing of it. But I, I was not going to put up with mine any longer. I knew I would never be a perfect human, but at least I would die trying.

What did you do? he asked.
I went out and got a haircut. Don't you like it?
No, I do. But it's very…different.

They colored it.

Colored?

Yes. To get rid of the gray.

That's what's different.

You think it's too much?

No, no, no. I just wasn't expecting it, I guess. It looks very nice.

Every morning I inspected myself in the mirror, as if becoming acquainted with a stranger. I liked the woman I saw there, and wanted to learn more about her. Did she have a long past that might take years to unravel? One full of unanswered questions, or buried thoughts? I became fascinated by the connection I had with her.

At the same time I felt distant, as if I were watching a movie or reading a novel that featured this alter-ego of myself. Though I was drawn to her, I wanted also to assert my real self—the one I knew I was becoming.

TOM

She became oddly amusing, and by turns irritating. I was happy to see her coming out of her shell, but her new, unpredictable nature had the strange effect of making me uncertain about who I was. It's funny how you can get accustomed to relating to others, each in a different way. And when you detect a person changing it throws you off course. Anne had been throwing me off course for some time, but now it took a new pitch. I felt she was challenging me to become someone else too, though she seemed unaware that she was doing it. I wasn't sure what I thought about this new Anne, but I knew I couldn't walk away from her.

I noticed she was taking early morning walks, almost every day. And that was good for her. She always returned in good spirits, sometimes humming. At times I would catch a melody, and it was familiar. I ended up humming along with her. Then, one day, it struck me: we were humming church hymns. Where had she learned them?

I go to Mass every morning, she said.

And they still sing those hymns?

Why wouldn't they?

They're very old. Remind me of my childhood.

Oh, are there newer ones?

Yes, but I'm not as attached to them. But—why have you been going to Mass?

I don't know. I'm finding something there. Something I didn't know I had. I think I want to become a Catholic.

Really? I mean, why?

Is it a problem?

No, it's not a problem. You can do it. Anyone can do it. But it's a long process, I think. I don't really know though since I was born one.

Any why don't you go to church?

I do go, sometimes. I don't know why I don't go more often. I guess I don't see it as necessary.

I see. Maybe I have the wrong idea about it then.

Your idea is a fine one. Don't let me influence you on this. If that's what you want to do, do it.

ANNE

I think they thought I talked too much, though I never said even a tenth of what was on my mind. I guess it's what my mother had taught me, to question everything and make sure I understand something before moving on to the next thing.

One thing I learned was that religion is full of hidden meanings, and my mentors weren't always keen on discussing them with me. But I was usually able to find them myself. Sometimes I talked about them with Tom. At first he was reluctant, saying he just didn't know. But I could tell he did know, that he had thought about the answers to my questions. If it weren't for him I might have given up on becoming a Catholic.

I felt new inside and out. When I walked out the door and met the world, its freshness overwhelmed me. I began to recognize that the trees, birds, moles, and skunks were symbols of a deeper understanding of our world, a puzzle. I was busy reconstructing it. I saw everything humans made in the same way. Our neighborhood held as many keys as the woods and lakes surrounding it. Some days I was light-headed.

This light-headedness spread from my head to my heart, my shoulders and arms, my legs and toes. It spread to everything that was deep inside me. I think that's why I didn't know at first that I was pregnant.

TOM

It was so sweet the way she told me. How could I be angry, or shocked, or scared, or anything? She seemed so content, as if nothing could go wrong. Yet I knew that a lot could go wrong at her age, never having been pregnant before. Anne had a way of deflecting negative feelings about anything. She was above all pragmatic, but embracing of the not-so-good along with the good. So I didn't mention my concerns. I let the doctor do that. I trusted he would lead her in the right direction. I was surprised though that she came back nearly in tears after her first visit.

Well? I said.

She sat down and looked past me. It was that look she'd had just after they condemned her house.

The doctor had listed all the possible complications, and said they would do an amniocentesis to determine whether or not the baby would have Down's Syndrome. He also laid abortion on the table as an option.

I don't want to do either, she said.

But the amnio—

It might harm the baby.

They are very careful.

No, I don't want to do it.

But then we won't know. (I was surprised that I had used the word *we* for the first time when referring to the pregnancy.)

Some things you just have to trust. And I feel that the baby is fine. I's our baby, Tom.

At that moment I felt so many words percolate up the back of my throat, but I said none of them. I was caught between reason and, I guess, love.

Her term passed uneventfully, but then came a long, difficult labor. They considered doing a caesarean, but the baby finally crowned and was born: a fragile little girl, a bit premature but not enough to keep her at the hospital. So we took her home and kept a close watch on her, her tiny eyes struggling to stay open, her tiny heart beating visibly beneath her skin. We named her May, after the month she was born in.

Anne tended to May with the precision of a skilled nurse. She rarely called the pediatrician for guidance, read no books on the subject of child-rearing, and gently chastised me for holding May the wrong way or being insensitive to the various cries she made. Anne was simply, to my amazement, utterly focused and selfless as a mother. I was surprised, then, that she still took the time to go to Mass.

ANNE

It's both wonderful and unsettling to see so much of myself in little May. I can think of nothing but the excitement I've had watching her grow and develop, I think because I'm sure her discoveries of this world will be as acute and breathtaking as mine were. Already I note how she smiles and takes a deep breath when she feels a breeze rolling over her skin, or the way her arms move when the sparrows flock into the forsythia bush.

I'm finding the same peace when I'm with her that I find at Mass. We are lucky to have such a pleasant child. She is so keenly interested in what's going on around her that she doesn't have time to be annoyed, or to annoy us!

Cindy, who lives on our street, asked me to join a mothers' group. We meet at her house to talk about the business of bringing up children. I mostly listen. I can't offer opinions on the books the others have read. I do read books, but not those kind. I read to May too. Even if she doesn't yet understand what I'm saying, I'm sure she is hearing the stories in my voice. Cindy says I am doing the right thing. She read that somewhere.

They are already talking about schools: where to send their children. Not just elementary school, but kindergarten and pre-school as well. There seems to be a pecking order of schools that I'm not aware of. I wonder if Tom knows about it. When I think of little May going to school, my heart sinks. What can she learn there that I can't teach her? How could I leave her out of my sight for all those days, all those years, when I know we will not always be able to share that time? I want to be able to answer every little question she might have. I want to see the puzzlement on her face, and then the realization, the joy of making sense of things. I want her to add up all the explanations I give her to amount to a positive view of herself and the world we live in. Isn't that what all mothers want?

TOM

Anne is still in the habit of attending daily Mass, and she is taking our little May, now a toddler, with her. A couple of times I went along, but for some reason I felt like an intruder in Anne's world. And I am the one who was raised Catholic. I just don't have the heart to tell her that I'm not sure I believe in it any more, that when I'm at Mass I am thinking of anything but. Maybe it's because I feel bad about it. In a way, I've let myself down, or I've let my upbringing down, my Catholic ancestors. I know this is a personal struggle of mine, one I can't burden Anne with. Could it be that I admire her for holding on to it, like a nun in a black-and-white movie from the past? It seems so strange to me. I can't come to terms with it.

I've overheard Anne talking to her. Occasionally May responds, but usually she is just listening, very intently, as still as a sitting bird. But May's eyes are not as blank as a bird's. They drink in, analyze, and sort through information as it passes to her heart, where I am sure it stays.

Once, as I walked down our driveway to fetch the lawnmower from the shed, I overheard Anne's soft voice explaining the lives of caterpillars to May:

The caterpillar wraps himself up in a nice blanket and goes to sleep. Then he wakes up and crawls out of the blanket and he's not a caterpillar any more. Now he's a butterfly.

But where does the caterpillar go?

He doesn't go anywhere. His body changes so he is now a butterfly.

Does it hurt?

I don't think so.

But why?

Why? Because that's the way nature thought it should work. We don't know why. We're just here to see it.

Is the caterpillar dead?

Not really.

Why did my hamster die?

Because he was old and sick, and living things have to go away some time.

Mommy, am I going to die?

Anne took a moment to collect herself:

Yes, honey. But not for a long time.

But then I won't see the butterfly.

Maybe you'll become a butterfly!

Is that what happens after you die?

We don't know exactly. But if you want to be a butterfly, maybe you can be.

I want to die today.

No, no, no. We don't pick the time when we're going to die. That's God's job. And besides, I'd miss you!

But if I'm a butterfly I can come and visit you.

You don't need to visit me, because you live here with me.

Anne recounted this conversation to me later in bed. She started out matter-of-factly but then became visibly shaken.

The poor little thing! Worried about dying! I wish I had better answers to give her. I feel I'm not a good mother.

Anne—there is not a better mother in this world. And besides, those kinds of answers don't exist.

But how do I explain an afterlife?

I don't know. How do you explain something we're not even sure exists?

It must exist. I know it must exist. It's not something I can explain, that's true, but I could never deny it.

We speak in metaphors with children. Either that or we just regurgitate what some religion tells us, which is a kind of cop-out.

Why do you say that?

Because if you don't understand something deep down, then you don't understand it.

But isn't that where faith comes in? she said.

Faith. To have faith you need some kind of foundation.

What if that foundation is love?

How do you mean?

What if you find that deeper understanding in other people, and together you create faith, based on that camaraderie that I'm calling love?

Is that what they're teaching you in catechism class?

No. It's just the way I feel about it. You don't have to make fun of me.

Sorry. I didn't mean to. And have you felt this kind of universal love your whole life?

I don't know. Maybe I did, even if I wasn't around people that much growing up, and I didn't know what to call it.

ANNE

Emma said God knows when I'm going to die, May told me one morning, out of the blue.

Emma was one of the Eucharistic Ministers at the church. She was a kind woman, soft-spoken, with a certain light in her grayish eyes. One thing about Emma though; once she started talking you couldn't get her to stop. She would go on and on about something, and if it was a response to one of my questions about the Church, she'd go on oven more. I always listened, then I'd go home and think about what she'd said.

Emma took a liking to May. She volunteered at the school where May was in Kindergarten, and May drew pictures for her. I sometimes invited Emma over for dinner, and she stayed with May a couple of times when Tom and I went to the movies. When May started first grade I was finishing up my catechism training. We invited Emma to the Mass that celebrated my entry in the Catholic Church. I could see her beaming from my vantage point on the altar platform. Emma was so happy for me. She felt she was gaining a new member of the family.

Emma was also a gardener, and she would stop by to swap perennials with me, or offer a new tip for controlling pests. She seemed more confident and knowledgeable than Tom's neighbor Olivia, who would stop by and just shake her head. When Emma and I worked in the garden together I felt a close bond, as if we had been cut from the same mold, even though our backgrounds were so different. She came from a working Irish family that had suffered many misfortunes, including the deaths of three of her four sibling before they had turned thirty. One was killed in Vietnam, another by a drunk driver, and the third took her own life. Emma, being the youngest and shy by nature, took refuge in the Church to contemplate these fateful incidents. She found that she didn't have to come up with the answers alone, that there was a whole tradition that dealt with such things, a tradition that would guide her through the pain and loss she felt.

It pained me too to hear her tell of her family. I wanted to offer her something. I looked for something to say, but I found that she was not in need of condolence. She had come to accept what had been given to her, and she was at peace with herself.

Once, when Emma came over to help me plant a river birch tree, she offered that her sister had liked birch trees, and that if she had been with us she might have helped us choose the best location for it.

Maybe she is here with us, I said.

No, Anne, I'm sure she is in heaven. She was the kindest person I've ever known.

But how do we know where heaven is? Couldn't it be universal, not just somewhere up in the sky?

It isn't here. I know that.

But look around you. There is a bit of heaven here, right in my garden.

It can be heavenly, yes. But it's not heaven.

What's the difference?

Heaven is not of this world. I thought you had catechism!

I did. But much of that is metaphor. Don't you think?

No, I don't.

There are times when I genuinely feel I understand heaven. I don't know that it's a place really. It's more of a perspective, an attitude. Maybe a feeling. It can happen anywhere, to anyone.

Oh, nonsense, Anne. Where do you come up with these ideas? I hope you're not talking to May like that.

I try to reach her as a child, I said. Whatever that may be. I'm comfortable revisiting my childhood with her, and seeing things the way she does. I want to make her comfortable in this world, not afraid of it, or of what may come next.

During May's schoolgirl days I would take her to my childhood haunts—the woods and fields near our condemned house, which lay in ruins. My beloved gardens had turned to weeds, but miraculously we'd find a random tomato or cucumber plant that had self-seeded. I would explain to May how things grew, but I got the feeling she was listening vacantly. I could never tell what she was thinking. I think she preferred soccer practice, or trips to the ice skating rink with Tom. They always came home laughing together. It was then that I finally realized: May was not me. She would keep to her own path in life, and I would never know intimately where that path led.

TOM

May loved to dance. Her ballet teacher said she was very disciplined, but that she was also given to divergence during lessons. That's very nice, I'd hear her instructor say, but it's not what we're doing right now. In pre-adolescence those little divergences became more frequent.

I took her horse-back riding, and it was a pleasure to watch her handle her horse with confidence as she navigated trails through fields and woods. She was just as much at ease out of doors and she was in. In her schoolwork I'd see her sit without distraction to complete an assignment she enjoyed, be it algebra, science, or music. But if she didn't like a particular lesson at school, she would fidget in her chair, text her friends, or simply stare out the window for long periods of time. Her teachers told me her grades were inconsistent. But one thing was clear: she was not the kind of kid who was out to get her parents, or challenge us constantly. She never said no to me, and with Anne she was respectful and loving, though sometimes unsure of herself, as if she had no clue about Anne's expectations of her.

Then, at fifteen, May changed. Anything she might have harbored during her childhood surfaced. Feelings flew from her mouth like daggers. Nothing Anne or I could say would go unchallenged. When I began losing my temper with her I decided to send her away for a summer. She stayed with my brother, the gentleman farmer, and his wife, in Vermont.

When I called there Janet usually answered. Brian was constantly busy renovating, feeding the animals, or digging up something. The report Janet gave us was always the same: May was having a good time and learning everything there was to know about the farm. She was courteous and helpful, and weeks passed before I decided to check in on her again. But before I could I received an unintelligible call from a girl whose voice I did not recognize. She spoke in staccato, her words thin and shaky:

I don't know where Dylan went. He took the car.

Who is this?

I need to get home. They left me here.

Is that you May?

They left me here. No. I'm not. I'll call you back.

I dialed her phone number but she did not answer, so I tried again, three more times, before she answered. But she did not say hello. Instead, I heard other voices in the background. They sounded like police officers.

Hello? May? May? What's going on there? Can you hear me?

She hung up. I tried calling again, and after several rings an officer answered her phone. He said the paramedics were taking her to the hospital.

ANNE

Tom and I didn't say much during the drive to Vermont. We were able to contact the hospital after Dylan's mother, Susan, had called to tell us where to go. Susan related that her son and May had eaten a piece of some kind of marijuana bar, but that it had affected May more strongly. Susan was at the hospital with May and Dylan. She said they were running some tests. She did not sound frantic, but hesitant. I told her we were grateful that she was there with May.

When we arrived we found May in a hospital bed, looking at us as if she knew who we were but she didn't quite know what to say. Even as I hugged her, she had a confused smile on her face. A nurse came in and checked on her, but was cold with us. I didn't know what exactly was going on. Tom began asking the questions.

What happened?

We're having some tests done, but it looks like bath salts to me.

What's that?

The latest street drug. It can cause psychosis.

Dylan, who hadn't yet said a word, spoke up: No. We didn't take any bath salts. It was medicinal marijuana.

Medicinal?

Here.

He produced a wrapper that still contained a piece of what looked like a candy bar.

Where did you get this? Susan demanded.

My friend Mack gave it to me. He's being treated for cancer and he takes this for nausea.

She glared at him. Then the nurse spoke up:

Can I see that?

Dylan handed it to her.

The thing is, you never know where this kind of thing is coming from, or what's in it.

May's eyes darted back and forth. It looked as if she didn't trust any of us and would have bolted from the room if she could.

I had to step out. A feeling of loss overwhelmed me. I had lost my daughter. I didn't know if she would come back. I would never have left my mother. Even in my darkest moments of adolescent confusion I sought her for comfort. Was that so unusual? Why hadn't my daughter looked to me the same way?

Excuse me, said the nurse, who found me alone in the hallway. Your daughter should be fine to go home, but I'd keep an eye on her for the rest of the day.

The ride home was quiet, so quiet it seemed we were driving through another world. I'd turn my head to catch a glimpse of May, who sat in the back seat looking out the window, her expression ricocheting from a smirk to terrified to helpless. Tom drove with both ease and determination. I felt cut off from both of them, and sought comfort.

Thank God it wasn't worse, I muttered.

God had nothing to do with it, May replied.

We need gas, said Tom. We have less than an eighth left.

It was a long country road, but luckily we were approaching a small town, and the next intersection had a convenience store with a couple of fuel pumps. As we pulled in I noticed a small church next door, a Catholic church called Saint Anthony's.

I'll be right back, I said, opening the car door. May watched me walk away and enter the church.

It was not a remarkable church: undecorated white plaster with wooden beams along the ceiling, clear window panes inset with leaded outlines of the Stations of the Cross, a wooden altar with a large crucifix hanging behind it. I picked up a church bulletin and read on the cover: *St. Anthony, Patron Saint of Lost Things.* I quickly said a prayer while sitting in a pew, listening to the wind find its way through a window that had been cracked open. The stillness quieted my nerves. I don't know how long I sat there. But then my heart jumped in my throat; I had left my child behind. I felt selfish and disoriented. How could I have done that? In my panic I rose to leave, but there came a hand on my shoulder. It was Tom's.

Are you ready to go?

Yes. But you left May in the car!

She's fine, dear.

No, she needs us. What's wrong with me?

We walked back to the car and I opened the back door to give May a little kiss. She looked at me, but there was still distance in her eyes.

TOM

Weeks passed before our house began to feel normal again. And yet I wasn't entirely convinced that it was. Anne's doting on May was met by May with some suspicion, and many times

I wanted to tell Anne to hold back, but she seemed to be in a delicate state too. So I said nothing. I was also aware that May was much more accommodating with me than she was with Anne.

Anne's friend Emma dropped by often. I think she sensed we'd been through something, so I finally told her what had happened. Emma had that quality of looking both interested and aloof when you spoke with her, like someone who doesn't quite understand your language. I always had trouble finding things to talk about with her.

Anne was more polite with Emma. They shared an interest in gardening, and among other things, religion. But while Anne was quiet about her new-found conversion to Catholicism, it seemed that Emma couldn't stop talking about it. She invited Anne to Catholic activist groups, and Anne attended them more out of a duty to friendship than anything else.

Emma thinks we are too lenient with May, Anne said to me. She had just returned from a Catholic Life meeting.

What does she think we should do? I answered.

Take her to church more often. Her confirmation is coming up.

I don't know that that would have any positive effect on her. She is who she is. As long as she knows we are here for her, the rest is—I don't know—

Maybe I'll take her to the rally on Saturday.

Rally?

The Pro-Life rally at the clinic.

You're going to that?

Emma says we need all the support we can get. Why don't you come?

I don't think so. I don't know what I think about it. I'm not sure it would be a good thing to take May there, either.

Don't you think it would help focus her? Let her get out-side of herself?

Maybe. Be careful, Anne. It might backfire.

What do you mean?

I mean, we need to give her some room to figure herself out.

ANNE

I had never been to a rally before, of any kind. I realized after we'd gotten there that I am really a shy person, and thought it might have been a mistake to come. But Emma made us feel welcomed. She introduced us to some of her friends, who did not seem to be very unlike me. May mostly observed; she did not want to hold a sign.

It was a chilly day, and there was plenty of hot tea and coffee to warm us. At one point it rained lightly. Patients moved through us on their way to the clinic, which offered, among other things, abortion services. I could see they were taken aback by us, but they kept right on going to their appointments. I wasn't sure how I felt about it. Was I being confrontational?

I caught the eye of a young woman, probably no more than twenty years old, with blondish hair that fell partially over her face. I smiled at her and she walked away from me, slowly turning her gaze toward the entrance. Then she fell to the ground.

I rushed over to help her, feeling a sudden cramp in my right leg. I rubbed my hand over it and felt that it was wet. Wet and red with blood. I heard loud voices converging, some screaming, other shouting. The girl who had fallen tried to raise herself, but couldn't. The others had backed away. I could see a group of men wrestling with someone on the lawn beside the walkway. Someone picked up a hand gun that had fallen there. My leg burned. But all I could think of was May. I couldn't see her in the crowd.

TOM

The second I saw lights flashing down the road ahead of me I sensed something had happened at the clinic. They'd had threats before, so it was only a matter of time. I sped up a bit, but when I reached it I saw they had blocked the road. I counted four ambulances. Paramedics seemed to outnumber the protesters, who huddled on the sidewalk, away from the building.

I heard Anne before I saw her. She was calling me from inside one of the vehicles. She was in tears.

Where's May? Where's May? I can't find May. Tom!

They were bandaging her leg. I took her hand.

Are you okay sweetheart?

It's my leg. A bullet went in me.

She'll be fine, said the paramedic.

But May. Please, Tom—

Yes, I'll find her.

When I turned around I found that the police had cleared the area in front of the building. Yellow tape girded the walkway and lawn, and forensics was already at work. Even the onlookers were dwindling, and Anne's ambulance was the last to drive away.

I stood feeling hopeless and scared, as if I had been thrown into a foreign war, unsure of whether or not I'd be able to communicate with anyone. A police officer asked if I was all right, and would I move off to the side. What's she look like? Look like? She's—she's—. Okay sir, I'm trying to help. Could you please describe your daughter. Never mind. I see her right over there.

May had appeared at the corner of the building. She had been crouching behind a line of spreading yews. She slowly approached me, and began to cry. I held out my hand and she took it. The officer left. When I tried to hug her, she pulled away from me.

Mom? she said.

She was shot in the leg. They took her to the hospital. They said she'd be okay. Let's go.

During the drive neither of us spoke. May sat in the back seat, staring out the window with one hand on the door handle, as if she might escape. She sat there, frozen, until we reached the emergency room. When we arrived I had to open the car door for her.

The waiting area was crowded, but quiet, except for a television that blared a news program. May stayed near the door as I approached the desk and told the receptionist who I was and who I'd come to see. After a few long moments a male nurse came out to lead us to Anne's room. I was surprised to find her alone.

Where's the doctor? I said.

They've already bandaged me up. The bullet just grazed me. There are others in much worse shape. May, honey, come here.

May approached the bed and Anne took her hand.

Where *were* you honey? I couldn't find you.

I was afraid. I didn't know what to do.

Thank God you're okay.

God should have protected us.

You're upset. Tom?

Let's be glad we're all here and we're okay.

Other's aren't, May responded.

We brought Anne home, and I was surprised how absolutely calm she had been during this ordeal. Two of those who had been shot that day died.

May disappeared to her room; I could hear her talking on her cell phone to her friends. She was crying. I tapped on her door and asked how she was doing. Fine, she said. I'm fine. So I went downstairs and got to cooking dinner But I didn't get too far before Emma came knocking at our door.

Tom, I heard. Are the girls okay?

May's fine, but Anne had a bullet graze her leg.

I'm here, Emma, Anne called from the couch. I'm fine, really.

Emma walked over to give Anne a hug.

And May's okay too?

Yes.

What a horrible thing. I don't know what's wrong with this world.

What's wrong is that people can't accept that not everyone thinks the same way they do, said May, who had come down from her room on her way to the kitchen.

What do you mean? Emma replied.

May did not respond.

I think she is kind of down on religion, I said. Understandably so.

No, no. It's not religion that caused this violence, Emma called out.

Anne replied: May is right. You can't expect everyone to have the same point of view.

Really? Anne? But we do all need to have the same point of view! We need to help guide people to the Lord's message, that we are all one.

We can be one, but we can't help coming from different places Emma, and seeing things a little differently.

I didn't like where this conversation was going, so I excused myself. Said I was going for a walk. I stopped in the kitchen, where May was rummaging through the refrigerator, and asked her to tend to her mother while I was gone.

I walked as if I were heading to the drug store, which wasn't very far away. But I really didn't need anything there. The direction I took was more out of habit. What I really needed was a bench to sit on, preferably in the midst of trees. I doubted such a place was near. But I kept walking.

I turned down a side street that I normally had no use for, and after having walked down that quiet street for half a block I noticed a pathway between two houses. There was a sign affixed to a tree trunk there; it read *Stevens Woods.* I had heard of Stevens Woods but had never made it a point to find it, though I knew it to be nearby. I also knew it contained a pond where neighborhood kids could ice skate and play hockey. Hockey season was now at an end though; it was mid-April. Tomorrow would be Easter Sunday. The air was a bit too chilly for a walk in the woods, but I followed the path in, hoping not to find anyone there but myself.

A stray crocus bloomed here and there, probably the offspring of someone's backyard. Squirrels thrashed through the floor of dried leaves. I hadn't gone far before finding the perfect fallen tree trunk to use as a bench. I sat there, and noticed a hush fall around me, as if all the living things of the woods were suspicious of why I had come.

It was the conclusion of Holy Week, and I had not realized that until now. I had done nothing to commemorate or celebrate it. As a child it would have consumed me both in body and spirit: the fasting, the imposed silence, the church not quite as full as on Sundays, and darker for evening services. The Stations of the Cross painstakingly visited, their focus suffering and death. The priest washing the feet of twelve chosen parishioners on Holy Thursday. The stripping of the altar. The quiet. The reflection. The bond I shared with so many others, all agreeing to follow these traditions, not dwelling on how they came to be, just recognizing the bond, the tacit agreement we had to recognize their validity.

And now here I was, a different person, a foreigner to that distant boy, sitting in the woods on Holy Saturday, thinking about Anne.

How different we were, like two species from distant planets. No matter how much we had grown together, our childhoods would always remain irreconcilable: hers innocent, pantheistic, and trusting; mine tied to unshakable traditions anchored in a global super-family that prescribed human relationships that were above considerations of the natural world. And yet Anne's sense of moral responsibility was no less than mine, and though she had grown toward the more coherent model, I had grown away from it. It was as if her pantheistic sense had rooted her and allowed her to believe in the intrinsic good in people, while I was growing to doubt the religious systems that people had developed as holding us back from a more natural good. Was that why I loved her? Did I want to believe in her innocence as mine was failing?

There, in the spring woods, I felt strangely out of place, even if I was welcomed. I felt ashamed for having left Anne at home, an innocent convalescent, as I had embarked on a selfish little trip of reflection and identity crisis—a crisis that could be never-ending, inconclusive. So I stood up, kicked away the dried leaves in my path, and headed back home.

ANNE

May was upset with me; I could tell. She averted her eyes when speaking to me, and would not spend more than a few seconds in my presence. If I asked her to make me a cup of tea, she brought it with my favorite jam and toast on a wooden tray. Then she scurried away. Why don't you sit with me? I'd say. But she always had something to do, somewhere to go. It made my heart ache.

Tom had gone for a little walk, and when he came back I could see he was not present. I was beginning to feel invisible in that house. So I said something that surprised me; I don't know where it came from:

Tom, I'd like to go on a little retreat.

A retreat? To where? Why?

I don't know where yet, but someplace where I can reflect.

Can't you do that here?

It's not the same thing. I'm too involved in your life and May's.

Anne, are you saying you want to separate?

No—I'm saying that I just need some time to re-anchor myself in this world.

Will you go to a monastery? Father Meyer can recommend one.

I don't think so. I need a break from religion too.

But you're not okay. And May—

I'm not hurt that badly. May is okay with it. In a way I think she welcomes the idea.

I see. Teenagers.

That's part of it. She needs to find herself too. She feels more confident and centered around you, I can tell.

I don't know if I like that. Feels like I'm driving a wedge between you two.

You're not. It's normal. We have to let it go for now.

Maybe Emma could stop by while you're gone.

I don't think that would be a good idea.

Why?

Emma can come across as heavy-handed, even judgmental.

You're right. But I'll miss you. When do you want to go?

Next week? I'd like to find a place—I don't know—maybe in the country.

ANNE

It's not easy having your head in three places at once, living in all those worlds simultaneously. Every time I blink I don't know which one will emerge. There is the world I grew up in; that's the one that is always in the background, a phantom that flickers behind everything I do. It comforts me, but it also disturbs me, as if it is trying to tell me something but has no voice. Then there is the world of my new family, the rock of Tom and miracle of May. They awaken me and keep me focused. The Church does the same; it reminds me that I am part of a human-wide family, that there is nothing I have to go through alone, or without a network of support.

Then there is the third world, and that's the one I am looking at right now. I'm sitting on the back porch of this inn. Before me is a grove of trees, a little stream, and beyond them, a field. Then the mountains. Behind me is an old colonial building, white, half-filled with other guests. Behind it is a small-town Main Street, sparsely populated with locals, it not being high tourist season yet.

I am struck by the quiet, struck to find that I am alone on this porch, that no one else is out here with me. Do they have better things to do, or do they not find the view pleasing enough? Or maybe I am only here because my leg is still healing and I can't walk too far. Or no, I am here because I want to be no other place right now. I have community at my back and wilderness before me. I am in the middle.

I am struggling with guilt. Guilt that I am just sitting here while there is so much to be done, so many things wrong that need to be righted. Shouldn't I be out there voicing these concerns, which are everybody's? Shouldn't I be playing my responsible part in the human saga?

And yet, I know that what I am doing right now—which might appear to be nothing—is the right thing. I know it because I have lived a full life, and the richness of that life deserves a bit of reflection. Otherwise how will I ever know how to proceed?

Sitting here I feel protected. I feel Tom's gentle hands on my back and hear his kind words. I feel May's little hands curling around my neck. I hear her first words, then I hear her teenage voice quiver as she struggles to define herself while pouring it out to me. But I also feel a different kind of protection. I think it comes form the sky and the swaying trees. It comes from the rain and wind and snow. It comes from the dirt I pat around my tomato plants, and it comes from the tomato plants as well. It comes from the air that envelops me each day. It's another kind of love, constantly tapping me on the shoulder to remind me that it's here. I could not go on without that kind of love either.

I don't know how long I was sitting there, but I began to hear some chatter in the drawing room behind me. It seemed all the guests had returned at once. They greeted one another, stood talking in twos and threes for a bit, then took seats on the sofas and end chairs. Some kind of meeting was about to begin. I watched them, wondering who they were and what was going on. Then a woman chanced to look in my direction. She caught my eye, and waved me in.

Clearly these were not guests, but locals. The innkeeper had given them a place to hold a town meeting. I think they assumed I was one of them. I took a seat beside a gentleman who looked extremely limber for his years. I noted that his hands had seen much labor.

Gradually then it dawned on me: this was a meeting of local farmers and their families. From the seriousness of their faces I could tell something unpleasant was happening.

The town, I learned, was considering selling off a large tract of the nature preserve to a developer who had plans to build a resort spa. The nature preserve had originated with a family who had lived in this town since colonial times, with the stipulation that it not be touched as long as someone from the family was alive. The last descendant had recently died.

A network of mountain-fed streams ran through the preserve. It had been the undisturbed home of all manner of wildlife for generations. What's more, the farmers depended on those streams, after they issued from their protected source, to irrigate their fields. The developer wanted to tap these streams for a network of heated pools and fountains that would severely deplete the amount of water left for the fields. On top of that, the townspeople felt very attached to their beloved preserve and didn't want to see it ruined. The clincher, of course, was that the resort would bring in more tourists, more business, and more jobs for the town. Who could argue with that?

Well, plenty of people, as I witnessed.

I had nothing to say, but found the dialogue interesting and disturbing. I found myself in the middle of a fateful conversation that would decide whether others would be able to gaze on the wilderness I had gazed on earlier, or even be able to walk in it. It amazed me that we had such power, even if this was nothing new. I had seen the results of human decisions to overrun and control nature my whole life, but I had never come face-to-face with such a decision. It frightened me.

God gave us that land, one elderly woman said, so that we may revere Him, not so that we could turn it into a vain playground. People can go to the cities for that.

It wasn't God who gave it, returned a young man. It was one family who did. Now we have an opportunity to give it again for the greater benefit of our community. That is also God's will.

God's will? I thought. What was God's will? Who in their right mind could ever figure out God's will? God's will was that we came to be here on this planet with the power to oversee it, but never master it. That's a tough position to be in. It would be much easier to be a hummingbird. They only have to fly thousands of miles up and down the globe twice a year.

Because I didn't know anyone in that room I was reluctant to speak up. But the young man who had just spoken must have sensed that I had something to say, even if I had no idea what that might be. He locked eyes on me and reached a hand in my direction.

Pease ma'am, he said.

I'm only a visitor here, I hesitated to say. So I'm not sure my opinion is worth much.

I think your opinion might be very valuable—and unbiased, he said.

She's not a farmer, a voiced called. I felt obligated to respond:

I have been a farmer. I was home-schooled by the land, and the lessons I learned from it have been the most important lessons of my life.

Then you agree with those who don't want to see the resort built?

No, I can't say I am in agreement with that point of view. My intimacy in caring for the Earth and its plants gave me a peace of mind I couldn't have found anywhere else, but that peace of mind, I've discovered, is really useless unless I can tap into it in my relations with other people. We are a part of this Earth, but we are also part of one another. And that's a great responsibility.

Does being part of one another mean we can destroy the planet?

Building a resort won't destroy the planet. I'd rather not see the preserve go, but if you don't do something to save this town, there won't be anyone to enjoy it. There must be a way to build something responsibly.

What about my farm? the elderly gentleman said. They don't give a damn about me.

This man had blue eyes filled with both energy and sorrow, the kind of beauty that can only be borne of constant struggle. It didn't seem right that he should have to face this at the end of his life. I was beginning to think I had said too much.

The meeting ended quietly. It seemed evident that the developers would win. I left feeling uneasy about the whole thing because deep down I didn't quite know what I thought about it. I called Tom later that day and told him about the meeting, but he didn't seem to be aware of the crisis these people were facing. He dismissed it as a parochial inconsequence, which irritated me. I needed a few more days there.

The next day I took a drive through the countryside, hoping to ease my mind. Hills rolled away from the road, beyond the wide valley on both sides. I noted the absence of human habitation, then realized that I had been driving towards a national park. Fields gave way to a tall, dense thicket of trees; the road started to wind. I saw a large sign ahead of me proclaiming the park's entrance. And just before it, by a narrow side road, stood a produce stand. Its bright colors broke the more subtle shades I had been seeing. I stopped, pulling in beside one other patron, who was about to pull out.

I'm Anne, I said as the old farmer turned to face me. Rich, he replied, a bit startled. We recognized each other at the same moment. He was the farmer I had heard speak at the inn.

I saw you at the meeting, I said.

Oh yes. Some meeting, huh?

His hands re-arranged asparagus and rhubarb as he spoke.

I'm just passing through and happened to be there. It's an unfortunate situation for everyone.

I guess so. I'm not so sure the young people give a damn. People like me are caught between a rock and a hard place. The crazy weather we've been having isn't make it any easier either. Sometimes I feel the town is against me. But what can I do? Them developers coming in here to wipe me out, just like that. It's not right.

I bought a bunch of lettuce—I don't know why, since I would be going back to the inn where I had neither fork nor plate. But I felt I needed to support him.

My drive through the wooded park was uneventful, but calming. At one point I parked and took a little walk through a pine grove, but I quickly lost interest when I saw how the trees thickened and began mixing with tall oaks. The young foliage was so dense it felt like dusk in there, and any little creak or crack made my heart jump. I was sure I saw a black bear from the corner of my eye. Weren't they harmless? I wasn't going to find out.

But I did wonder, standing there in that dense forest, what I was doing there. I had left my family. I had left myself.

I didn't know who I was, or what I believed in. I didn't like that I felt exposed there, an imposter of sorts, even if no one was watching. So I quickly headed back to my car, drove to the inn, and packed up my things to go home.

TOM

I think Anne was happy to be back, but I could tell something was different about her. She seemed guarded, quiet in a way that was not normally hers. Several times I thought of asking her what was wrong, but at the same time I wasn't sure if I was making it up. Maybe she was the same old Anne, but I was seeing her differently? Then I felt disappointed with myself for not being able to read the situation clearly. Maybe I was changing?

Do you believe in God? I asked her, immediately feeling it was a silly question to ask at this stage of our partnership. After all, what would the answer matter?

I've always known there was a God, she answered. I never considered it something that required belief. That seems so decisive and petty, and also a little arrogant, as if we could ever judge or rule on such a thing. Why do you ask?

Because I don't feel the way you do. I doubt the whole thing. God. Religion. Our reason for being here. It could be a hoax.

That would be a pretty unnecessarily complicated hoax. Don't you think?

I don't know. It might seem complicated to us, but it could just be the universe unfolding, with us little specs just being another insignificant part of it.

I don't feel insignificant. Do you?

I'm not talking about how you or I feel. I'm looking at the big picture.

The big picture includes how I feel. In fact, how individuals feel has completely changed the course of history many times, and may well change the course of this planet beyond anything nature ever intended.

But we *are* nature. Nature made us. We're not apart from it. Anything we think, say, or do is just another facet of nature.

I don't buy that, I said. Not when we have the power to destroy the whole thing. My natural instinct tells me something's amiss with that.

I was tongue-tied, but saved by May, who came downstairs in a panic because she couldn't find something—a t-shirt, or sports bra, or whatever. She accused me of not laundering it; then she accused Anne of running off to meditate without first instructing me on how to do laundry. But before either Anne or I could defend ourselves May was out the door, for a run I believe, as if the whole thing had only been a moment from my imagination.

The next morning I woke up at my usual seven o'clock, and was surprised that Anne hadn't risen earlier, as she normally did. I watched her lying there, her gentle breathing and beautiful profile, before gently removing myself from the bed so I wouldn't disturb her.

A half hour later, as I ate my breakfast, I heard May sobbing upstairs, punctuated by her trying to call my name. I knew it was about Anne.

They took her to the hospital in an unresponsive state, though she did squeeze my hand when I told her I loved her. Looking back now I think that moment gave me peace, and the courage I would need to lose her, for she never regained consciousness. The aneurysm had been severe enough to cut her off from us. She was gone within a day.

A priest had come by to give her last rights, and I hesitated at first, forgetting that Anne had converted. Or maybe it was that I didn't see the need, or the point? But May spoke up and said: yes, definitely, please. As he recited the prayers, anointing her forehead, I had a strange sense of having come full circle. The ritual comforted me more than I had imagined it would. It also brought May to tears, though she tried her best to hide them.

TOM

In the days following the funeral I had the sensation of traveling back in time. My life with Anne had been reduced to a dream, and I had trouble reminding myself that it had been real. Could I have made the whole thing up? Did I just return from her vegetable stand in my pick-up truck, another Saturday morning, alone, on my way to a predictable, stalled life?

Later that year, with May off at her freshman year in college, the house was more in order than I'd seen it in years. Everything that was placed there—the pillows on the couch, the newspaper, the kitchen utensils and pair of slippers—was placed by me. I walked through the rooms as if walking through myself, feeling both comforted and unnerved by it.

Within a few weeks I was attending Mass, first on Sundays, then occasionally on weekdays at sunrise. I sat there mostly daydreaming, just as I had done as a kid, and only being attentive to the readings if some line or another caught my attention. I usually sat far away from anyone else—the few nuns who normally attended, or elderly parishioners who had made it their daily habit to be there. I felt comforted, at least for the first few times, then I felt myself swinging back to skepticism and loneliness. I hadn't realized it earlier but Anne had grounded me in some way. She had kept me from feeling hopeless. She was a bridge for me: a bridge between myself and religion, between self-consciousness and defeat, and now between life and death.

I found her journals, those she had written mostly as a child, at a time when she had no religion, no formal training, no formal anything. And her words have haunted me since. I hear them when I am falling asleep; then they fill my dreams. They interrupt my morning coffee and change the course of my speech when I am talking with someone. Her childlike voice becomes womanly. She is always near me. It is all that I hear.

ANNE

When I'm an adult, I'll have all the time in the world. I'll take long walks through the fields and woods. I'll read whatever I like. I won't be afraid of anything, because by then I'll understand how everything works. If I can't find the answers in books I'll just figure it out myself.

When I'm an adult I'll never wear that boring face adults sometimes wear, the one that says, I'm just doing this because I have to. I'll never do anything unless I want to. I'll wake up in the morning and look out the window, and there I'll find another day's weather. By then I'll know how any kind of weather makes me feel, and I'll never be surprised or angry about it. Even if I am sick, I will know that it is just another day, and that days keep coming, and everything changes.

Today was my favorite day. I have a lot of favorite days, but this one was my favorite day so far. Now I'm trying to write down anything that happened, but it's not working. I can't think of anything. I just woke up, ate breakfast, helped my mom make applesauce, and took a walk. It's not even my birthday. Why is it my favorite day? It's just how I feel inside. I feel like I am as big as the world and everything in it. I went to my favorite tree, a really big oak tree, and sat there looking at the fields and hills far out. I could see the tall buildings of the city too, it was so clear. I was all by myself, but it didn't matter because I could still taste the applesauce and feel my mother's warm hands. The leaves shook above me in the wind, and it made me think of my grandfather. His hands were strong and not so soft, and he smelled good, like cigars.

It's spring and the purple flowers are blooming. Some animals have come out of hiding, especially the bunnies. There are always a lot of bunnies. Pretty soon we'll have some fresh lettuce to eat. We haven't had that in a long time. Everything that was dead is coming back to life, just like it does every year. It makes you feel clean inside. My mother says we will have a special dinner to celebrate. She bought me a special dress, white with pink and blue ribbons on it.

My friend Sarah who lives down the road is celebrating too. She calls it Easter. I went to her house on their celebration day. Everyone was wearing nice clothes, even her dad. They had come from church, where they listen to a man who tells them how to be good people. Sarah says they sit then stand then sit again there on hard wooden benches, and she gets bored.

Sarah and I were outside picking little flowers so we could float them in a bowl of water on the pretty table her mother was setting for dinner. We had violets, dandelions, and blossoms from the quince bush. Sarah also found some small blue flowers that looked like pin cushions. We were about to bring them inside when Sarah's father came out holding a brown paper bag. Sarah told me it was full of baby bunnies. From where? I asked. From our backyard. My brother ran over their mother with the law mower and now the bunnies won't live. What's he going to do with them? But Sarah didn't know.

He took the bag and put it inside his car in the garage, then drove the car out of the garage. He let the car run and got out, holding the bag. Then he held the opening of the bag tight against the pipe that comes out of the back of the car. He held it there a while, then looked inside the bag, then held it up to the pipe again. Sarah and I watched.

You kids get lost, he said. But we stood there until he waved us away again.

That happened yesterday. I lost my flowers on the way back home from Sarah's. I held my hands closed tight all the way, but when I got home there were no flowers in them. I went to my room and closed my door. I heard my mother coming up the stairs. Annie honey—are you in there? I didn't answer. I wanted to read. So my mother opened the door and came in. I was reading a book about spiders, studying their cute little faces in the close-up pictures. Mommy, I said, why don't we ever go to church?

I don't know—Why? Is there something you are missing? We can go if you want to.

No, I think I'd rather be outside. I need to protect the animals and spiders.

Protect them? From what?

From people who go to church.

She didn't say anything else, just closed the door and let me be.

About the Author

Mark Saba grew up in Pittsburgh of Italian and Polish heritage. He is a graduate of Wesleyan University and Hollins College, where he received the Andrew James Purdy Prize for his fiction as well as the Gertrude Claytor Poetry Prize, sponsored by the Academy of American Poets. He wrote his first novel as a senior thesis while at Wesleyan; at Hollins he became more interested in writing poetry as well. His first published novel, *The Landscapes of Pater*, tells the story of a young man in search of a father figure, including a journey to Sardinia to meet the relatives of the father he had never known. More recent works of his include *Ghost Tracks: Stories of Pittsburgh Past* and the poetry collections *Flowers in the Dark* and *Calling the Names*. Mark is also a painter. You can view his artwork and learn more about his publications at *marksabawriter.com*. He worked for 33 years as a medical illustrator and graphic designer at Yale University. His wife, Joan Saba, is a noted hospital architect. They have two children, Annie and Nicholas.